EDEN ALSON

The Novice Twins

A Novel

ARBITRARY PRESS
New York

This book was professionally typeset on Reedsy.
Find out more at reedsy.com

For
my Mom, my Dad, my Grandma, my Grandpa,
and for you.

Those who don't believe in magic will never find it.

- ROALD DAHL

Prologue: The Strangers of Dark and Light

The small bugs began to scatter, the cat slipped under the couch cushions, and everyone closed their doors. The starless night of witches had begun.

The first to emerge was a sky witch, and she pulled the bright sparkling lights out of the dark blue void. Then the others. Each took a star and swallowed it. Kilana the earth witch smiled. "The fun begins."

Each began their act of mischief, a few things here and there, plants became rocks, doors opened and closed, window panes became pure stone. The small town of Salem was a madhouse.

One witch stood alone, flicking her fingers at some flies, turning them into pieces of candy. Then she heard a cry, a baby's cry, nothing to be worried about.

But then she saw something. Stars flying out of an open window. Helga, the alone witch, a water witch, assembled the rest of the witches.

"Maybe one of the stars got thrown in the window," one of them speculated.

"Can we eat the stars?" asked another.

"What if there's a witch inside?" said a third.

The last one got the most attention. The witches were all aflutter over the idea. Then Helga volunteered to go up and look in the nursery window. All the witches thought this was a capital idea. Hilda floated Helga up to the window, and the water witch peeked in.

She saw a room decked out in blush pink, and a pale baby girl sitting up in a cradle. Stars flew out of the little girl's mouth. Helga's eyes opened wide, realization flickering across her face. She almost cried, but the other witches below demanded to know exactly what she was seeing. The baby girl smiled and reached for Helga's flowing, ocean blue locks.

All of the witches began to pull Helga the water witch down, frantically asking her questions.

"What's going on?"

"Can we eat it?"

"Is it another witch?"

Salty tears fell from Helga's eyes.

"Helga?" Kilana whispered in the water witch's ear. "What is it?"

Helga, distraught, whispered back. "One of my daughters."

The sky witch turned at this. She shook. Quietly she pulled a knife from her skirts and swiftly sucked all the color out of the world, throwing the knife into Helga's stomach while the water witch's daughter spewed stars.

* * *

Someone screamed as the first plane crashed into the tower. Everyone scrambled to get away. Except for a man behind the second tower. He had spiked dark purple hair and bright green eyes and white skin with no pigment. He smiled like something was funny about homicide. He pulled a dark holly wooden bracelet off his wrist, hearing a scream as the bundle in his cloak squirmed. Everyone around him was running, yelling fire. Sirens swirled. But he was in his own world, with a baby girl hidden in his cloak.

He disappeared into the second tower virtually unseen.

The first tower was falling. Many were already dead. Those that weren't ran and yelled like the world was ending. He supposed it wasn't unreasonable to think the world was ending.

Inside the building, the strange man opened the door of a broom closet and pulled out the squirming bundle from his cloak, holding her up, twisting a lock of her hair around his finger. The dark blue strand of hair pushed blood to the tip of his finger, making it red. The people fleeing the second tower barely noticed this relatively calm man and beautiful pale baby girl. They were in a chaos of their own.

If this didn't work, he'd be ruined, he'd be a dead man walking. But was this the right way to prevent it? With infanticide? With the murder of this helpless baby?

He watched the scene unfolding before him and felt the whole world shake. He placed the bundled little girl inside the small broom closet. Before he could close the door, she screamed at him and bright stars flew from her mouth.

He tried not to think or feel as he slammed the door and leaned against it, taking a deep breath. Before he could change his mind, he walked away, out of the tower, without looking back. Without looking back while his daughter spewed stars.

I

Summer

Cat

1

Enter Cat Novice

C at Novice was walking through the village. The heavy basket of laundry that she dragged behind her smelled awful and drew many unwanted looks from the townspeople.

Even the unconventional beauty of Cat herself was not enough to distract from the terrible smell, and the eerie air about her, the solemn gloom that followed her like a cloud.

In the town center, she gave up and sat on the side of a marble fountain. She dropped the heavy bag on the cobblestone streets. Her feet were aching and her leather boots were peeling at the toes. It didn't matter to Cat's mother that her daughter spoke six languages and had read nearly every book in the town library. Her mother wanted her for one thing and one thing only.

Laundry.

Baskets and bags of laundry, filled to the brim. The simple yet arduous task required walking to the other side of town, to the pond, washing, then dragging the clothes back. Over and over again.

And yet Cat did this obligingly, for anything was better than going to school, which felt even more oppressive than washing clothes. At thirteen, Cat was older than her years, unquestionably smart, undeniably pretty and exceedingly clever. Her eyes were a shade of green so brilliant they looked like bright green leaves. Her hair was so black it was blue, dark and thick like waves of night sky flowing down her back. She was pale, but when she got angry she turned an alarming shade of red. This quality, along with a certain rebellious streak, did not go over well with the nuns. The poor girl was constantly getting into trouble. Her answers to the thousands of interrogation questions were always along the lines of:

"*No, I don't* know how Sister Mary went blind."

"*No, I didn't* turn the midday winter castor oil into slug slime."

"*No, I didn't* bring pond animals with me to school today."

She was eventually sent home permanently and punished with ever more laundry. So each morning she put on a faded jumper, a crisp white apron and leather work boots, pulled her dark hair back with a pale pink ribbon and hauled bags of dirty clothes through town.

* * *

At the end of the day, while the sun set over the chapel, she dragged the last load home. Walking through town, with sun rays flying across the sky, she felt tired and dirty. Resting momentarily on the edge of the fountain, Cat saw a man come running through the village.

He stopped in his tracks near her, wrapped in a dark cloak and looking at her with eyes that were red and slightly terrifying. He walked up right up to her and reached for her hands. She kicked at his shins, then ran, the heavy basket weighing her down less than before. This was not the first time a strange man had tried to put his hands on her.

At home, she was greeted by her mother, who was waiting with a wooden spoon and a scowl.

You see, Mother never liked her daughter, because whenever her gray-blue eyes met the leaf green ones that tortured her so, her ego took a big hit. Her beautiful daughter was the opposite of her in every way, and it hurt.

"Cathrine! Where in Salem have you been?"

Cat was tired. She wasn't ready for another fight with her Mama. She tucked a raven strand of hair behind her ear and lied. "Sorry Mama, today is town laundry day. There was a very long wait."

"Oh." Mama almost seemed disappointed about not being able to whack her daughter with a wooden spoon, but in this small section of Salem, hitting your child without reason was an offense worthy of a jail cell. And while her mother wanted many things, she did not want that. So the wooden spoon went back into the pot of boiling brown stew.

Cat sat down in a nice armchair and took her fable book from the table next to her. She swung her legs over the arm.

"Go fill the metal tub. You're filthy. And then put on your night things. When the sun goes down it'll be the starless night of witches." Cat grumbled something about finishing "Brüderchen und Schwesterchen," but she walked out the back door and dragged the metal tub to the water buckets. The water would be cold. She also took some firewood and some rocks.

Cat slumped down next to the buckets and the metal tub. She leaned over the cool edge, and stayed there until she heard, "CATHRINE! WHY DO I NOT HEAR THE WATER?" Cat sighed and sloshed the first bucket of water into the tub. The water came gushing out and though Cat tried to shield her face, she wound up having to spit out a rusty mouthful of it.

By the time she finished filling the tub, numerous buckets later, the sun was turning the sky pink and orange and she was wet, tired, and still dirty. She lit a fire with some difficulty and placed the tub on top of it. Then she went inside.

Cat climbed to her room, shedding her clothing down to her underthings, then climbed out the back window. She slid down the ladder she had leaned up against the house. Landing in the garden, she sat on the patchy grass and hugged her knees to her chest. It had been a long day.

She had dirt under her fingernails, and her night-sky hair was matted and dirty. Her body was weak and heavy on her ankles, but she had to keep it together.

Cat's life was never easy. She sometimes wished she could just be swooped up into a different world. Little did she know, when she *was* swooped up, she would wish she was home again.

2

When Cat Met a Witch

That night, after Cat hand cleaned her hair and brushed it (with extreme difficulty) and scrubbed her fingernails raw, she choked down a few sips of something brown and gloopy that she was sure her mother had just made to torture her further.

Then, stomach rumbling and eyes bleary, she walked up to her room, pulling her faded white nightgown over her head. She took the pale pink ribbon out of her hair and splayed her dark hair over the pillow, slipped under her blankets and tried to fall asleep.

When she woke, the sky was dark. The stars had left the sky. But somehow, there was a deep purple glow in the center of her room. There, stood a woman with braided dark red hair that reached her knees and glimmering purple clothing. She had matching purple eyes and skin as pale as Cat's.

Cat leapt out of bed and snatched up the fire poker. She stood, shaky and scared, holding the poker like a sword.

"Hello, Cathrine," the woman said. Her voice was silky and strangely familiar.

Cat didn't scream. Just said, "Who are you?" barely breathing the words. The woman smiled in a kindly way.

"I am Kilana, an earth witch. I was your mother's best friend. I'm here to take you to the place where you belong."

* * *

Kilana only had to explain the fact that Cat needed no longer to live with Mama anymore, and the girl was up and packing.

Cat did love her mother, but to *live* with her and be used as a laundry slave, well, she was more than excited to leave. She filled her bag with dresses, aprons, and her few books. She pulled on her leather boots under her long nightgown.

Then, as if to prove that she was leaving, she reached to the floor and picked up the pale pink ribbon and pulled her hair back, saying, "Let's go."

In an eyeblink they were riding through the world on a black horse. When dawn broke, Cat rubbed her eyes and began asking questions;

"Where are you taking me?"

"What happened to my real mother?"

"Am I actually a witch?"

"Why are the buildings getting taller?"

Kilana answered all of her questions with some hesitations.

"You're going to The Academy, a school for witches. You'll get supplies when you get there."

"Your real mother was killed… by angry villagers."

"Yes, you are a witch."

"The buildings are getting taller because the witches have created a way to travel through time, so we are one-hundred years away from your time. I have a pamphlet of all the things that you missed, I'll give it to you when we get to where we're going ."

Cat's head spun. She wondered what exactly a pamphlet was, but she also felt unmoored, out of place. The horse's feet raced through the water.

They were now flying through a beach of... as far as Cat could tell, well, she couldn't tell.

She looked out to the beach, where women and men were floating in the water, and shouting at the horse. They rode for what felt like seconds and hours at the same time, until Kilana said, "I'll give you the pamphlet now, we're almost in 2018."

Cat quieted and sat still. Kilana grew worried after a few moments. "Are you okay?"

She was not, but she said, "I am fine, thank you Kilana," and stared at the pamphlet.

Everything was just so confusing.

When the horse came to a halt, the two witches were in a forest of dark green trees and Cat slipped off the back of the horse.

It was then she realized that Kilana was gone. She looked around for her friend but the warm purple eyes and long red hair had disappeared.

She clutched her bag in hopes of safety, but she found none.

Cat was alone now, and she didn't like it.

3

Enter Rosie Porter

Cat stood in the forest until dawn. She was getting very bored. She looked out into the trees and sighed. *Oh les peaux de pommes de terre.- Oh potato skins.*

She eventually stood and walked further into the forest. And as she went on, the trees became, well, different. The leaves turned lighter and lighter green until they were yellow, then golden.

Cat was in awe. Forests weren't gold. They were green and leafy or skeletal and barren. She was still looking up when something or someone tackled her, knocking her to the ground. Choking on dirt and grass, Cat saw that it was a girl around her age, who now lay on top of her, grinning like a monkey.

"Hi! Sorry!" squealed the girl. She pulled Cat up by her hands and dusted off her dress. "I'm Rosie!" Cat couldn't help but giggle. The girl was anything but a rose.

Rosie was incredibly beautiful. She had short lavender hair and lavender eyes that glimmered with mischief and were made larger by mint-green cat-eye glasses. She even smelled like lavender.

"I know, right, they had to name me after a *different flower*, too," said Rosie, rolling her eyes but still grinning. "You must be Cat."

" Y-yes, hello," Cat stammered. She was such a shy person that she flushed from her ears to her shoulders and was suddenly interested in a dirt stain on her boot.

Rosie held out her hand, and said, "Let's go down to The Academy, then we can talk about getting you some supplies, and modernize you." Of all the confusing things in that sentence, Cat decided on:

"Down?"

"Down," answered Rosie decidedly, taking Cat's outstretched hand.

The grassy ground opened up underneath them and they fell through.

* * *

Rosie squealed with delight and Cat screamed like a banshee as the two girls fell hand in hand through the nothingness. They landed with a crash in a room with shimmering silver walls made even brighter by golden streaks of sunlight streaming in. Cat was not one hundred percent sure how that was possible, since they were underground. Rosie's glasses were on the floor, but surprisingly not destroyed. Rosie picked them up and wiped the lenses on her shirt. She slid the curved ends behind her ears.

Suddenly a voice came through the open window. "Rosalina Porter, 1943, fire witch."

Rosie got to her feet and stood at attention. "Yes ma'am."

"Cathrine Novice, 1825, undecided."

"P-p-present," Cat stuttered, standing and brushing off nonexistent dust.

"You may enter The Academy."

Doors that Cat could have sworn hadn't been there a moment ago, swung open. The girls walked through.

Inside, was a room with glass walls and the largest most amazing and comfortable looking beds Cat had ever seen.

Rosie smiled, and said, "Welcome to our room. Headmistress thought it would be better if things were explained to you before you met all the other students. Also, you look like you might need a nap."

"A nap?" Cat said. "What is that?"

"This." Rosie grinned and lay down on the bed, closing her eyes. "It's when you go to sleep in the middle of the day..."

Cat lay down on her bed and closed her eyes just as Rosie had.

When Rosie opened her eyes to look, Cathrine Novice was already asleep.

* * *

Rosie was rummaging through the bag that Cat had brought with her a while later, mumbling things like "That's gotta go" and "who even has these anymore?" when Cat opened her eyes and sat up.

"Oh good, you're awake," said Rosie. "Do you have scissors, and sewing stuff?"

Cat nodded groggily.

"Oh, here it is," Rosie said, digging to the bottom of the bag. She began threading needles and snipping with the scissors. Cat was too exhausted to help her or stop her for that matter. After watching from the comfort of her bed for a while, Cat finally got down on the floor and started helping Rosie make her old Victorian wardrobe into a modern one.

They cut up dresses into pants and shirts or shirts and skirts, and Cat happily threw her petticoats and slips out the window of their small room. They were making horseback riding clothes, when Headmistress Hilda came in.

4

Headmistress Hilda

"**H**eadmistress, Hello!" said Rosie, standing up and bowing slightly. "This is Cat. The new student. We were just modernizing her wardrobe."

The Headmistress smiled warmly. She was a kind woman, her golden hair streaked with silver and arranged in a tight top knot. She had dark eyes and dark, slightly purplish skin.

"Oh good, Rosie, can you bring your project over to that corner there while I have a little chat with Cat here."

Rosie picked up the fabric and sewing things and left the Headmistress and Cat alone.

Cat had been overflowing with questions, and finally there was someone to answer them. She started with the most obvious. "Where exactly am I? And why?"

"When a witch comes of age," Headmistress explained calmly, "as you did last week when you turned thirteen, you start to develop a flame, the source of your magic. Later, when you develop an element, your hands will glow and your flame will be easier to take.

"The demons will notice, and try to take your flame. So The Academy is the one place the demons can't find you. A safe place where we can teach you how to handle your magic."

As far as Cat was concerned, what she'd just heard was a bunch of words that didn't really make much sense. She took a deep breath. Maybe it would be better to think in practical terms. "What supplies do I need? Because both Rosie and Kilana mentioned that?"

"You'll need a magic wand, of course, and books, dance shoes, dance outfits and some horseback riding things. It should all be in here." Hilda reached into her swath of silver clothing and pulled out a small blue velvet purse no bigger than Cat's fist.

Cat couldn't stifle a laugh. "That! It's barely bigger than my hand! How could it possibly fit everything you just described?"

Hilda chuckled softly. "You'll see. Any more questions? I'm on a tight schedule."

"Just one. How have you been alive so long? Kilana mentioned how long you two have been friends."

"Witches die when they choose to die after they turn thirty-five."

Cat thought about this, biting her lip. "So how old was my mother when she died?"

"Thirty-three," said Hilda.

Cat felt her heart skip a beat. "Oh."

The only sound that could be heard then was the snip of Rosie's scissors.

"Well, I'll leave you to settle in and look through your class schedule," Hilda said, handing her a sheet of paper.

Cat choked back a sob, but her eyes dried instantly when Hilda walked through a purple circle in the wall that disappeared the second she went through.

"Oh Cat, I'm so sorry," said Rosie.

Cat took a deep breath. "Don't be. Now, are we making night clothes?"

"Yeah, you should change out of *that*," said Rosie, pointing to Cat's grass-stained and slightly tattered nightgown.

"Um, sorry if this is rude, but how long have you been wearing that?"

Cat could barely remember. The last few days were a blur, the travel, the people, everything she'd learned. She smiled and said, "Two-hundred *years*."

She and Rosie collapsed into fits of giggles.

And for once in her life, despite the hole where her mother had been, Cat Novice felt like she was home.

* * *

The next morning, Cat woke to the sun shining in her eyes. She hadn't been in school for many months. While they got dressed, Rosie went on and on about how nice the kids in their classes were. Cat listened but had her doubts.

She wore a skirt made of the thick black material from the dress she'd worn for her her grandfather Dewy's funeral. Her only memory of him was that he smelled like peas and pepper and was always complaining about Jefferson and how he "ruined the country." For a top, she made a sleeveless number out of a nightgown her mother had given her for her tenth birthday.

Rosie bounded up behind Cat and smiled, handing her the pale pink ribbon. The girls both laughed.

"So what exactly is *finding your element 101*?" asked Cat, falling back on her bed and holding the paper schedule over her head.

"Um, well, every witch has powers related to an element. But not the normal kind of elements, the witch elements." Rosie stumbled through the explanation. "Fire—that's my element—water, sky, earth, and time. The class is to find your element. And when you do, they give you this little symbol." She pointed to a shield-shaped symbol with an image of a blazing fire in front of a purple background emblazoned on her palm.

Oh, Cat thought.

"It doesn't hurt," added Rosie, seeing Cat's face. "It seems you have Professor Oy for that."

Cat's eyebrows went up.

"Oh, yeah, there are warlocks here, too. They teach mostly." This helped but did not answer Cat's unasked question about her new teacher's strange name.

* * *

When the girls arrived at the main hall, they quickly got on line at the breakfast station. Eggs, fruit, and something Rosie called French toast, the whole thing drowned in maple syrup and whipped cream. Cat hadn't eaten in days, and she piled her plate high.

She smiled at Rosie, who took thin crispy pieces of bacon and added them to the mountain of breakfast food. They sat at a table and began to eat and talk, and for a while, Cat thought that maybe her life here could be normal.

But then she saw Jamie, and all that changed.

5

Enter Jamie Novice

For Cat, it was like looking at a mirror. The girls were identical in almost every way. Although there were stylistic differences. Cat's hair was long and neat, whereas Jamie's hair was chin-length and messy, with light blue strands streaking through it.

They were both pale, but Jamie's skin was white. No peach pigment in her skin at all. They were both thin, but Jamie's bones looked like they would slice through her skin. Despite this, their eyes were the same, and when they locked, there was an instant of stunned recognition.

Cat was frozen over her breakfast mountain. Jamie just stared, mouth open. Then her eyes narrowed ever so slightly, just enough to be noticeable to Cat, and she turned away. Cat went back to dismantling her breakfast tower and Jamie ate alone, and the two girls tried to ignore the knot that was now binding them.

* * *

The *Finding your Element 101* classroom was crowded and thick with dust. Unfortunately, Rosie had graduated to *Controlling your Element 101*, so Cat was there on her own. She sniffed the air and tried to determine the smell. She'd smelled it before. Est-ce que c'est du Alcool? She coughed. Then Jamie walked in.

They looked at each other in surprise. Jamie held herself up a little bit, and tucked her hair behind her ear and walked to the back of the room, or rather the top. The room was slanted to the sky, and the solid, flat ground was as big as one of the floors in Cat's house. It was the largest room Cat had ever seen.

As all the students gathered, Cat sat in the middle. No one seemed upset or put out that the teacher had not arrived yet. Cat frowned and looked at the spread-out floor. There was one porcelain tub for every two students, and just as many piles of wood kindling.

Just as Cat was wondering why there was no water, the door flew open.

The person who came through the door was the furthest thing from Cat's image of a professor. The class fell silent, and Cat had to squint and make sure she was seeing right. He was tall and thin, with floppy gray hair, a goatee, a dark fedora, and no eyes.

What should have been his eyes were covered by a thick black gauze, and he was holding a large bottle of golden liquid. His mouth was fixed in a scowl, and if he had any joy in his heart, it was not to be seen. He took a long swig of the drink.

Ah, thought Cat, *Donc c'est ça l'odeur.*

The professor set his bottle down. "Gud Mornink students, I am profezer Oy."

The other students seemed absolutely unfazed by their teacher, but Cat was agog. This was the strangest class she'd ever taken.

"Velcome to findink your element von oh von, please hand over your vands."

All the students grumbled and reached for their wrists. And they each pulled off a wooden bracelet and handed it to the professor.

Cat remembered Headmistress Hilda mentioning the wand, which was in her little purse. She felt through her pockets, then pulled out the blue velvet purse.

She reached into the purse and was surprised to find that it was practically bottomless.

She found three pairs of shoes, and then a wooden stick, which she pulled out with great difficulty—it seemed to be lodged in between a pair of ballet slippers and a riding helmet.

She looked at it. There was detailing on the handle of symbols, which Cat guessed acted as a barcode (she loved that word, which she learned in the pamphlet). She wondered how it became a bracelet.

Suddenly, professor Oy was standing in front of her desk.

"You ave not anded over you vand."

The other children looked at Cat.

Her eyes widened. "How-" But Cat handed over the wooden stick. The professor snatched it out of her hand.

"Now zen, pairs. Everyvone please find a partner."

The class scrambled to pair up. Soon every child had their arm hooked through someone else's arm. Everyone except, Jamie and Cat.

The girls looked at each other with distaste.

"Gurls, please partner up and join ze group."

Cat reluctantly tried to hook her arm with Jamie's. Jamie wouldn't let her. The girls walked over to the group, where the others were choosing their porcelain tubs.

The professor sat in a quilted high backed chair, swung his legs up on the desk, and took a swig of the golden bottle. "Now. Choose a tub and go-go." He lowered his fedora over his... eyes and leaned backward.

The children started running around and picking up the wood and moving the tubs. Cat was very confused.

She was scared to say anything to Jamie because her companion was terrifying beyond reason. The sharp features and sharp eyes made Cat look away.

"Uh. So, shall we begin?" asked Cat, offering a weak smile. Her companion looked her, with eyes primed to kill. Cat almost felt a knife slice through her. "Um, or not."

Jamie began moving their tub. They both stood next to the tub and frowned down at it.

"You take the wood, don't set it on fire too much," said Jamie dryly. She walked over to the other side of the tub. She held out her hands and began to focus on the bottom of the tub. No water pump or buckets and nothing to light the wood.

Just then, Cat realized something.

What she was supposed to do was light the wood on fire with her mind.

Oh, potato skins.

6

Finding Your Element 101

As a schoolgirl, Cat had faced many difficult tasks, from writing lines on her slate to arithmetic. The schoolhouse hadn't been kind to Cat. But of all the tasks assigned, she had never been asked to set fire to a pile of wood with her mind.

The students had begun to fill their tubs with water. Jamie was filling theirs one inch of water at a time. She was so concentrated that Cat thought her eyes would pop right out of her head.

Fire was much trickier. Cat looked around the room with helplessness. One girl had her nose stuck in a book entitled, "One hundred and one ways to create things out of thin air." Cat looked at the wood in front of her, focusing very, very hard on it, imagining it bursting into flames. No luck.

She looked over at Jamie. "Um, can we switch?"

Jamie shook her head violently. She stared back at her three inches of water. Cat frowned.

The other children had started to boil the water in their tubs. Cat could almost feel their thoughts mocking her. She could imagine the wood mocking her. Then it did. Very very loudly, the wood laughed at and teased Cat.

A pile of wood had somehow grown a mouth and begun heckling the poor girl. Professor Oy pulled up his fedora and stared. The other children laughed like hyenas.

"Vat is this?" asked the professor, his face angry.

Cat shrunk.

"You are worthless at magic!" yelled the wood.

"Be quiet," said Cat and tried her best to imagine the wood without a mouth. It didn't work. She felt a tear leak from the corner of her eye. The wood finally shut it's stupid wooden mouth.

Cat felt so stupid. She blushed from the tips of her hair to the tips of her toes. She went back to trying to set the wood on fire, and Jamie went back to her three inches of water.

* * *

When a strange squawky sound filled the classroom it meant class was over. Cat practically ran into Rosie's arms in their next class, Dancing, Cooking, and Other Human Skills.

She described her run-in with Jamie, her incident with the talking wood while Rosie held back giggles, nodding seriously. But at last she couldn't contain herself any longer and bellowed with laughter. But a moment later, the smile slipped off her face.

Approaching the two girls with alarming speed were three identical-looking girls. There was literally not a single difference between them. Each had tightly braided hair that was dark purple, smooth skin the color of cocoa beans and dark purple eyes. Each also had a smattering of dark freckles across their noses.

They stood before Rosie and Cat with smirks on their faces and hands on their hips.

"Who," said the first girl, "Are," said the second "You?" said the last.

Cat pointed at herself with questioning eyes.

They nodded in unison.

"Oh, um, Cat. I'm new."

"Cool" said the first.

"I'm," said the second.

"Violet," said the last.

"Brennan" added the first.

Cat was about to ask which one of them was Violet Brennan, when Rosie interrupted.

"Are you girls here for any reason, or are you just taking up space?"

The girls all shot her death looks, rolling their eyes in unison.

"Well," "We" "Have" "A" "Note" "For" "Cat," "But," "Always" "A" "Pleasure" "To" "See" "You" "Rosie," they chimed, deeply sarcastic.

The way they talked made Cat's head spin.

"Here" "You" "Go" "Cat." The girls all handed her a third of a letter at the same time.

"Uh, thanks," said Cat. She took it. They even all blinked at the same time. They pulled their hands back into the link they had. They turned around and walked away. Then they stopped abruptly and, turning their heads, said, "By" "The" "Way," "Cat." "I'd" "Be" "Careful," "If" "I" "Were" "You."

Cat cocked her head to the side, watching the girls walk away. Frightening.

Rosie just shrugged when Cat looked at her. "Maybe they just wanted to mess with you."

Cat put the pieces of the letter together and gasped.

"What?"

"I've been summoned to the Headmistress's office."

"Why?"

"She's going to introduce me to my sister."

7

Sisters–Sort of

After an eerie silence, Rosie said, "What are you waiting for?" And pushed Cat down the hall.

She arrived at the headmistress's office, hearing what sounded like two people having a screaming match on the other side of the door.

"I can't believe this!"

"Miss Novice. This is not up for debate. We've even taken samples. There's no doubt about the truth here."

Cat knocked on the door.

Hilda opened it and smiled calmly. She had the look in her eyes of someone who was both trying to keep herself from punching someone and keep someone from punching her.

"Headmistress, you summoned me?" said Cat, forcing her mouth into the smallest smile. Hilda ushered her in.

Sitting there in the office, eyes red and angry, was Jamie.

* * *

Once Cat had caught her breath, and Jamie had stopped trying to turn herself into a mouse, Headmistress Hilda sat them down.

"You in fact are twin sisters. You were both born in 1984." The two girls looked at each other and then whipped their heads back towards Hilda.

Hilda sighed. "Your mother, Helga, had you girls after her... husband... left her." Both girls raised an eyebrow.

"We don't know how you—Jamie—got to two thousand one, or how you—Cat—got to eighteen twelve—"

"Whoa whoa whoa," said Jamie, moving her hands in front of her,

"I was born in two thousand six. What do you mean two thousand one?"

Headmistress Hilda bit her lip. "So it seems that you both were brought to a place of danger and violence, of destruction and death." She looked at the ceiling.

"The war of eighteen twelve," said Cat.

"Nine Eleven," said Jamie. Cat wrinkled her nose in confusion. Both Hilda and Jamie frowned.

Hilda sighed. "Cat, darling, did you read the pamphlet?"

Cat blushed.

"I read most of it," she said.

Jamie leaned over, whispering in Cat's ear. Cat's mouth dropped open. "What! That's dreadful!"

Jamie nodded solemnly. "So how the heck did we survive?" asked Jamie, frowning.

"Your father," Hilda said, making quotation marks with her fingers, "found you, Cat, in the middle of a battlefield, and took you home. And

27

Jamie, one of our time witches found you on the top floor of building two of the World Trade Center when it was clear the building would fall. Seeing a baby, especially a witch baby, you were taken out of the building immediately and sent up around five years."

"Is that why I don't have a family?" Jamie asked. "Is that why I ended up in the system?" She looked on the verge of tears.

"I'm afraid so." Hilda took a look at the girls faces. It was clear they were both hungry for information.

Cat had always been kept in the dark, she knew nothing about her birth. But now that she knew something, she wanted more. Headmistress Hilda took a folder out of the stack of papers and opened it.

"It seems you have another sister. A half-sister who's nineteen, who ran away. No one's heard from her in years, but we know where she is. There are records of a daughter she had as well. She'd be about four or five now."

Cat couldn't breathe. She'd discovered in the space of the past five minutes that she wasn't an only child, but in fact had two sisters and a niece.

"Your half-sister lives in New York City 1984. Her name is Charlotte. Her daughter is Kitty."

"Have either of you ever noticed a man in a dark cloak with red eyes?" Hilda asked abruptly.

Jamie nodded. Cat had to think. Then it hit her like a bird against a glass window. She had, on her last day in her own time. She nodded.

"That man is a demon. He was looking for a witch's flame to take. Young witches like you two. That's why you were both taken to The Academy as soon as possible."

Jamie's face was stony. Cat's was both scared and still.

"Any questions, girls?"

Cat and Jamie looked at one another.

"Why did we end up in those dangerous places?" asked Cat.

"Someone must have sent you there."

"Who?" asked Cat. She leaned forward a little bit.

Hilda coughed. "We haven't been able to determine that."

The girls both frowned, looking at each other quizzically.

Jamie tucked her hair behind her ears and looked again at Hilda."Just one more thing, Headmistress. Who is our father?"

Headmistress Hilda looked extremely uncomfortable. "Um…your father, yes—" A loud croaky sound filled the room. "It's complicated. And there's the bell." Hilda pushed the two girls out the door. "Don't want to be late. This is your first day," she said, slamming the door shut behind them.

The twins looked at each other, sizing one another up. They could have been the same person, and yet Jamie was somehow rougher around the edges and angrier.

They walked to their next class together. Potions. "Well, that's pretty cliché," Cat said, looking at her schedule.

"Agreed," laughed Jamie. "I guess we must be sisters."

Cat smiled. "Guess so."

They both laid notes from Hilda on the teacher's desk while the other students stared at them. Then they found two seats together and sat down.

II

Fall

Jamie

8

Potions and Popularity

J amie stretched her fingers just a little bit, lifting up her toes up just a tiny bit more.

Why the heck, she wondered, fingers brushing the glass jar, would they put the dragon fangs so completely out of reach for kids? She sighed and slumped down from her stretched out position.

Jamie's five weeks in The Academy had sparked a love of Potions class. The Potions class was on the roof of The Academy, with open air windows, and light pooling on the ground.

She had been spending her afternoons after her classes in the potion room making magic candy with Rosie.

At the moment, while Jamie was trying to snatch the dragon fangs, Rosie was sitting on top of her desk, legs crossed and eyes closed.

Jamie was slowly falling in love with Rosie. She thought that she was kind and exciting, not to mention beautiful. But to all the other kids,

Rosie was weird. Which didn't at all bother Jamie.

But one day, walking through the hall (which was actually on the ceiling after a strange student turned the halls upside down and removed the gravity), she heard someone say, very loudly, "Only freaks hang out with Rosie Porter." Then a laugh, sharp, curt, and with a sneer behind it.

Jamie ran down the hall, blush creeping up her neck.

The girl who made Jamie blush was named Emily Kalna.

Emily was a bit like a doll. Her hair was like twisted curls of gold, her eyes were sky blue, and her skin was like marble. She was like the paintings of angels Jamie saw in museums. She reminded her of all the pretty girls she'd ever met. Emily had chosen a group of girls, all beautiful and doll-like, just like her. The three Violets were let in because everyone was scared to defy them.

Emily's right-hand girl was, oddly enough, Rosie's cousin Grace, a pretty girl with smooth chocolate skin and shoulder-length dark pink hair (like all of Emily's acolytes), who, for unknown reasons, hated her cousin Rosie, acting like she barely existed or had feelings. But then all the girls who wanted to be part of Emily's group went to great lengths to make her happy lest they be kicked out or fall into disfavor. Each semester, Emily chose seven girls to be a part of her group and made them just to her liking, all of them wearing the same style clothes and getting similar haircuts. All except the three Violets, who were not made to straighten their hair and cut it to their shoulders simply because of how terrifying they were.

Jamie, for her part, refused to become one of the girls who cut their hair like Emily's or complimented her shoes. She was too stubborn. And cared about Rosie too much.

* * *

Hours had gone by. Rosie was gone. Jamie left the potions classroom. The sun was setting over the forest of golden trees and Jamie was walking around, trying to find Cat and Rosie.

Finding Rosie was easy. She was leaning against a wall, talking to a girl with orange and blue hair and eyes that shone when she saw Jamie.

Cat was harder to find. They had to go to the forest of golden trees, and it took a while to locate her. She was in one tree with shining gold leaves, on the very top, with her legs dangling over the branches.

They called up to her, but she didn't respond, seemingly lost in her own private world. Jamie stared up and then Rosie lifted her by her waist. She swore as she got queasy but flew up through the air like a bird and landed, hanging upside down, her legs supporting her body. Jamie just hung there, waiting for Cat to grab her hands, to lift her, to help her.

But no. Cat just leaned against the tree, and took her bracelet off. She waved it, and it sprang back into a wand. Cat swished the wand, and a warm, sparkly cloud flowed around Jamie.

She floated up, and ended up lying against the other side of the tree. She swished Rosie up into the tree. Rosie did flips as she flew up. When she landed on the branch, she held her head.

"Man oh man, Cat, you need to work on your floating. I feel sick," Rosie said, clutching her stomach and waiting for the punch on the shoulder. But it didn't come, and then Rosie saw why.

The three girls were looking at a dark pink sky, with streaks of orange and yellow, and the most beautiful blood red sun, like nothing they'd ever seen.

They all bowed their heads before the setting sun and grabbed each other's hands, holding on tight, waiting for the next moment to arrive, secretly wishing the one they were in would never end.

9

Demon Dreams

Jamie ran, head pounding, blood rushing in her ears. Her bare feet hit the ground, her angry teeth ground together. Her whole body was aching and she knew she had to stop. But there was no way she was going to stop, not if it meant that *It* could catch her.

Up the path she saw Cat walking toward her. She yelled, "Cat, *It's* coming! Run!"

Cat turned, confused. Then in half a second, something came out of Cat's mouth, a dark, purple cloud.

It flew out of her mouth, her nose and her ears. Cat shuddered, and slumped down onto her knees, and then fell face down onto the ground.

It was clear to Jamie. Her sister, who she'd just found, was dead. And *It* was to blame.

Jamie screamed, then shot up out of bed, face wet with tears. Her door slammed open, and Cat flew into the room.

"Jamie!"

"Cat!" The sisters embraced. They collapsed against each other.

"I dreamed—"

"You died, oh Jamie—" They explained their dreams, and cried some more. It was strange to them, that just weeks ago, they'd hated each other. But now their past and their present joined them. They were forever linked. No one could cut the knot now.

Jamie and Cat lay down next to each other. As Jamie closed her eyes and drifted off, her body loosened. She slept. They both did. Quietly, and this time (thankfully) dreamlessly.

* * *

When Jamie awoke, she was next to Cat, and Cat was asleep. Cat smelled like wood and lavender. Jamie supposed it was Rosie's lavender perfume smell (their whole dorm smelled of it) but it felt good to think her sister smelled like her favorite flower.

Lying in bed, staring at the ceiling, Jamie wondered about their older sister. Did she have these kinds of dreams? Did her daughter? Was she even alive? Would she be able to comfort her?

Cat woke up after a while. "See you at breakfast," she said.

There was a moment of silence in which Jamie couldn't remember what Cat was talking about.

"Oh, uh, yeah, see ya."

Then Cat left. There were tear stains on the pillows. Jamie got dressed. She pulled out some itchy weird sweater, olive green and magenta. She was about to put it away when she felt a pang in her heart.

She remembered she had brought it with her from her home. She pulled it on and crossed her arms. She pulled on some tight black pants. She looked at herself in the mirror.

Her hair was sticking up all over. She picked up a brush and moved it towards her head. She tilted her head in the mirror. She placed the brush back down. She pressed her hair down with her hands, which did exactly nothing.

Walking to breakfast, her bones ached. Everyone was chattering about the upcoming sports tryouts.

"What sport is it?" Cat and Rosie were talking, and Cat was wondering about the chatter.

"Volleyball. I think it was invented in eighteen… ninety three?" said Rosie, drumming her fingers on the table. "After your time anyway." Her clothes looked like they'd been inside a paint factory that exploded. Tie-dyed t-shirt, bright pink pants, mint green glasses. She was almost too bright to look at. But that didn't stop Jamie from staring. Rosie rolled her eyes.

"I'm aware of how crazy I look. It's my only athletic outfit."

"I actually think you look cool," Jamie said.

Rosie grinned, biting off the fatty part of the bacon. "Thanks! So are you gonna try out?"

"Sure, why not?" *What am I saying?* Jamie thought, piling fruit on her plate. *I can't do sports!* She looked at Rosie hopefully, thinking, *it can't be that hard.*

10

Tryouts

Jamie went back to her dorm before the tryouts. She changed out of her sweater and pulled on a t-shirt and some looser pants.

She brushed her hair up into a short ponytail, then picked up her pale blue ribbon, using it to tie her hair. Jamie studied herself in the mirror. Despite having absolutely zero athletic talent, she *looked* like a sports person.

Violent flashbacks from her middle school volleyball unit were coming back to her as she walked to the athletic field. Getting beaned in the head, arms aching and hands hurting like heck. Her stomach spun.

All the girls trying out were gathered in the field. Rosie and Cat were clumped together in the corner, talking. Cat threw her head back and laughed at something Rosie said. A bump of jealousy settled in Jamie's throat.

Jamie had known that she was gay since she was four, when she'd declared to her foster mother that she was in love with her "Beach Barbie." She'd known she liked Rosie since the day they met. She wanted to tell her, hug her, hold her hand—dare she even say it—kiss her. But she couldn't. Not without freaking her out. She'd liked other girls before, but when she'd confided in anyone, they told her it was wrong, it was bad. Bullies, teachers, even her so-called "friends." Once, she'd been kicked out of a foster home for telling her foster mother.

"Feelings like that are impure, and they should be kept to one's self." The words rang through her head every time she looked at a girl. She again wondered about her older sister. Would she love her, even the way she felt?

Jamie felt her head swim and her stomach churn. She walked over to Cat and Rosie and made a fake smile attempt and waved.

"Oh! Hi Jamie!" said Rosie, smiling. *She doesn't have to fake it, her smile is always perfect. It never looks fake.* Jamie grinned involuntarily, feeling stupid, knowing she looked just as stupid.

Emily was standing with her group of minions, and the three Violets, who were spectators instead of players, but were on the field just the same. The rumors were that Emily was the favorite for team captain, but there were other girls who looked much better suited for the role.

There were two other girls in particular who looked athletic and leaderish. Option one was in Emily's gang, so she had no chance of being captain (if she was captain she'd be out), but she had midnight black hair, dark eyes, a short ponytail and athletic looking legs and arms. Jamie thought she was very pretty. She (like all the Emily clones) had a white tank shirt tied at the waist and bright pink shorts.

The other girl wasn't *in* Emily's group but she seemed to be one of Emily's future recruits (she was standing next to the group). She had red hair that was long and curly. She was wearing a blue tank shirt tied at the waist and yellow shorts.

She noticed Jamie looking at her and waved, walking over.

"Are you Jamie?"

Jamie nodded, wondering how she knew.

"You've been the hot gossip for months, you and your sister, um, Cat?"

"Yeah, why is that, exactly?"

"Cuz, you're the first twin witches to be born in different times, like ever."

"Oh, um, yeah, so who are you?"

"Oh, my name's June." She stuck out her hand. She had perfectly manicured nails and a blinding smile. Jamie shook her hand.

"June!" said Emily, waving her over. June shrugged, like, "What are ya gonna do?" and walked away. Jamie smiled. She waved at June. And mouthed, "I hope you get captain!" June nodded. Emily whispered in June's ear.

Jamie moved back over by Cat and Rosie as the coach arrived.

"Girls, straight line!"

The girls complied. Immediately.

Coach Marvlyn was a woman in her early five hundreds. She had shocking orange hair in a short bob *a la* the nineteen twenties, and electric blue eyes and thick orange eyebrows. She smiled slyly at the girls and walked up to Grace.

"I hear you've been on the team every year. In fact, you've been captain. Well, you know what I think about all that experience?"

All the girls shook their heads.

"USELESS! WHAT MATTERS HERE IS WHAT YOU KNOW NOW! NOT WHAT YOU KNEW IN THE PAST!"

All the girls trembled.

"SO GET OUT THERE AND GIVE ME FIFTY LAPS! NOW! I DON'T WANT TO LOOK AT YOUR FACES! GET RUNNING!" All the girls bolted out on the field. Even Cat, who probably didn't even know what laps were.

Oh dear, thought Jamie.

Jamie liked running, actually. She liked the ache in her thighs, lungs burning. She always had good endurance and good speed and was the first one finished with laps.

"Ya think you're tough?" Coach asked her.

Jamie nodded, her mouth in a straight steely line. Coach came so close to Jamie's face that Jamie could tell what she'd had for lunch (BLT sandwich, chicken soup and some kind of nasty energy drink).

"Yes, ma'am"

"Good genetics?"

Jamie shook her head.

"Then what, girl?"

Jamie still wouldn't answer.

"Do you know what lap the former team captain is on?"

"No." Jamie shook her head. *Lie.*

"Lap forty two."

I knew that. Jamie didn't respond, smirking.

Coach sighed. "Just do fifteen sit ups." She rubbed her temples and mumbled, "I need a coffee."

Jamie did fifteen sit ups. Then, when the other girls still hadn't finished, she did fifteen more. She was feeling pretty good about herself.

That euphoria lasted until they set up the net and she remembered she needed to play volleyball. The girls divided into two teams. June was on her team, but Emily and the midnight-haired girl were on the other team.

Jamie gulped.

Rosie looked really nervous. Her knees were shaking.

Cat, on the other team, frowned at Jamie.

Oh boy. This'll be fun.

11

It and the Game

The other team served first. Jamie had to bump it back to the other side. She threw her arms out, with her eyes closed, hoping to miraculously make contact with the ball.

Somehow the ball did hit her forearms and fly over the net, smacking right into Cat's head. But Cat seemed unfazed.

"Sorry," Jamie mouthed.

Cat shrugged.

June hit the next serve. June was the best player in the game, slamming her serves, winning them point after point. The game continued okay until the Violets got involved.

The three Violets had been watching from the sidelines, and were wondering what kind of trouble they could stir up. They all pulled out their wands and pointed at a ball that was about to hit Jamie in the head.

Jamie knew it would hit her, but her concern turned to terrified horror when she realized the ball had turned to solid stone.

Jamie cried out, trying to duck out of the way, but the sudden weight change made the ball come down even faster, big and heavy and gray. Jamie screamed just before the ball hit her on the head. The other girls screamed too. Then everything went black.

* * *

When Jamie came to, she was in a white room with a white bed and white bedding. She looked around. She felt her head. It had bandages wrapped around it, but underneath the bandage she could feel a huge lump, and when she touched it there came a searing pain like there was a fire in her skull.

Suddenly, a woman she'd never seen before burst into the room. She looked like an older version of the Violets. She had dark purple curls but softer. And dark eyes. She was wearing a white lab coat and a light blue shirt.

She smiled wide.

Ow. Jamie winced.

"I'll get your friends, they've been in the waiting room for the three days you've been here."

"Three days! Is that how long I've been out?" It made her head hurt to yell, but Jamie decided it was worth it. The nurse nodded. She held up a finger and walked out the door.

Jamie collapsed back on the pillow, closing her eyes. *Ouch.* When she opened her eyes, Cat and Rosie were in front of her. Cat burst into tears. It looked like she'd been up crying for days.

Rosie also looked like she hadn't slept in days, her already messy hair sticking up like she'd jammed her finger in an electrical socket. Her lavender eyes were wild and rimmed with red.

Rosie flung her arms around Jamie, her lavender perfume wafting, making Jamie more groggy than she was before.

"I missed you," Rosie said, "I was afraid you were dead!"

Jamie laughed. She didn't mean to, she just snorted out a giggle.

Rosie wiped her eyes. "What in the world is funny about my fear of you dying?"

Jamie was full on barking with laughter. It made her head throb like crazy, but she loved laughing like that. So it was worth it.

"It's just I," Jamie snorted. "get hurt," she fell forward, "all the time! And I never have any damage!" She laughed like a maniac. Everyone in the room, including the doctor, frowned.

"She's still a little delirious from the medication we've had her on," said the doctor. "I expect she'll be a bit groggy for the next few days." She turned and ushered them toward the door. "What she really needs now is to not be overstimulated. We'll leave you be, Jamison."

"Jamie, not Jamison," said Jamie, giggling.

"Uh huh," said the doctor.

As Jamie collapsed back on her pillow, she felt another laugh well up, but she stifled it, closing her eyes and falling back to sleep.

* * *

Jamie walked through the forest of golden trees. The dome sky was a light purple. She smiled at the moon, shining and bright. Then she saw something move through the trees.

It, she thought, and shivered. The dark purple cloud came up to her face, and *it* flew around her head.

"Jamison, Jamison, do you want your friend back?"

Jamie frowned, and turned around. She watched *It* move around her. All the light in the woods disappeared. "Friend?"

"Your friend, Jamison. The one with the lavender, her hair, her eyes,

her smell."

Jamie flushed. "Why do I need her back? I've got her already."

"You'll find out, Jamison. Until then, I'll leave you with this." The cloud spun until there was a girl standing there. Not just any girl. It was Rosie. She had a little ponytail in the back of her head. She grinned at Jamie.

Jamie reached out her hand. Rosie grabbed Jamie's hand. They held each other close. Hugging, hearts thumping. They moved away, and Jamie whispered, "I won't let *It* take you." They leaned close to each other.

Then Rosie disappeared. Just as the moment was about to happen, Rosie was gone.

"I promise you Jamison, when she matters to you most, she will be gone." *It* was back. The cloud was in front of her face again.

Jamie screamed,"What have you done with my friend?"

"Friend? Well, someone's in denial."

Jamie blushed, and said, angrily, "You haven't answered my question!" Her tears flowed, heavy waterfalls.

"You will see, Jamie. You will see." *It* poofed out of the woods. The only thing left behind was a pair of bright green eyes.

12

Rosie and Jamie Running Through the Trees

Jamie shot up out of bed and saw Rosie sitting by her bedside. She flushed. Her body felt weak, and her head hurt. She felt groggy but there was one word that rang through her ears loud and clear.

Jamie.

How did *It* know what her nickname was? *How? How?* It was dark in the room, and Rosie was reading by the light of her wand.

"Hi Jamie," said Rosie. "You talk in your sleep, you know."

Jamie almost cried, just to make it worse, all the things that she felt, and all the strange visions and *It*.

Rosie grinned at her in the dark, "You kept saying, 'It' and yelling at something." She shook her head happily. "I guess you saw that horror movie a few times, huh."

Jamie chuckled awkwardly.

"You also said my name," said Rosie, cheeks flushing. She giggled awkwardly. "I guess you have ESP or something."

Jamie sat up and looked at Rosie.

"Or maybe not."

Jamie knew that right then she had nothing to lose and absolutely everything to gain, so she leaned in and barely brushed her lips against Rosie's. A bolt of electricity shot through her body.

Rosie pulled away immediately. She stood up and ran out of the room.

* * *

After a month, Jamie was finally let out of the witch hospital. Cat visited her seven more times, and Rosie didn't visit her at all. It hurt, but she knew why. Cat brought with her anecdotes from Professor Oy's class, and news of how the three Violets got suspended. Nothing helped the wounds in her heart.

One morning, the nurse unwrapped the bandages and checked out Jamie's head one more time. Then Jamie was good to go. She had her first class, and Cat practically jumped on her when she walked in.

"I'm so happy you're back! I've been paired with Diana Delarosa for the past week, and she's so dull I sometimes think her whole life is in shades of beige."

Jamie laughed. She and Cat spent the whole class attempting to travel a few seconds into the future. In their next class, ballet, Rosie was there.

Jamie waved a little bit at her friend. Rosie grinned slightly but walked over to the barre. They were practicing their leg lifts by the wall. Jamie felt a pang in her heart. Cat tapped her on the shoulder.

"What was that about?"

Jamie shook her head. "Nothing. Let's warm up." Jamie wasn't going to tell her sister, not until she understood what was going on herself. (Plus, since she knew from Hilda that she was seventy seconds older, she felt responsible for her only family.)

Everyone did their ballet, and then took five. Cat rubbed her ankle, and Jamie went to sit by her. "You okay?"

"Just twisted, don't worry. Go see Rosie, she wants to talk to you."

Here we go, thought Jamie, standing up and walking over to her lavender friend.

"Hey."

Rosie smiled up at Jamie. "Hi."

Jamie sat down next to Rosie. They were sort of leaning against each other.

"So. You feeling better?" said Rosie.

Jamie just nodded.

"I'm really sorry, I just didn't know what I would say if I came back to visit you again."

Ouch, thought Jamie.

"It's okay. I just was afraid you weren't, I mean you didn't, I mean you wouldn't…" Rosie grabbed Jamie's hand.

"I get it." Jamie felt her cheeks heat up.

"But…"

Jamie's smile fell. "No it's fine. You don't have to apologize to me. But maybe don't tell Cat," said Jamie.

"Right," said Rosie.

"All right girls, back in," said the teacher. Rosie gave Jamie a tiny kiss on the cheek. They walked to the barre, and smiled at each other, as the music started, and they did their leg lifts.

13

Midterm Switch

S o they didn't tell Cat. But they had more important things on their minds. Midterms were coming, and the rules were strange and unusual. There was a note that had been passed out to everyone that read:

Dear Students,

As you all know, midterm tests are coming up. I'm listing the rules here:

~ You will be in groups of three or four (you will get to choose these groups, but they must be approved by me.)

~ On any given day, your group will be sent to my office and I will tell you what your task is.

~After your task, I will rate you on a variety of factors.

~Your grade will be a joint grade. No one student will get a

better grade in a group then someone else in the same group.
Good luck to you all.
Sincerely,
Headmistress

All the students thought the same thing. *Oh boy.*

Jamie, Cat, and Rosie knew they'd be in a group, but that was the only thing that was clear to them. Rosie was the only one who'd taken a midterm before, but she was no help.

She said the midterm tests were different every year, but this year was supposedly more intense. The older students were sworn to secrecy about what the events of the test were.

Jamie, Rosie, and Cat spent hours working on their magic for the tests. Cat's favorite was a spell that created a big glassy bubble you could move around in. She put Jamie in one, which was really bad. Well, for Jamie at least. For the others it was just a lot of fun.

"CAAAAAT!" screamed Jamie one afternoon, as she banged on the bubble. Rosie was on the floor laughing. Cat grinned as she moved the bubble around and stuck it to the wall.

"Cathrine Vanessa Novice! You get me down from here this instant!" Jamie shouted. Cat just laughed and turned the bubble blue. Jamie felt her skin tingle, and she screamed as she looked down at her arm. *BLUE!* Her whole body had turned blue!

"CAAAAAAAT!" She shrieked, banging harder on the bubble. Cat said something into Rosie's ear, and turned the bubble clear again. Jamie's skin went back to normal.

"We're still not letting you down!" yelled Cat. Jamie slumped in the bubble. She even ended up falling asleep. When she woke the bubble was gone, and she was on the floor, with a blanket thrown over her.

Rosie and Cat were still up and whispering. They were lying on their backs on their separate beds, talking and giggling. Jamie thought about her dorm. The walls were painted dark blue, with three windows. It was dark and cavelike. The whole room was both lonely and quiet. Not ideal for anyone except some kind of goth girl (which Jamie was not, really).

She had no roommate, but there was a girl who left after a few days, cracking under the pressure. But she had been weird anyway. Oddly enough, really goth, midnight black hair, pale skin and so on. It was odd she didn't like it there.

Jamie thought about this room. She liked having her friends close by, and she liked the windows as walls that let light in during the day and drew in the moonlight at night.

She liked the sound of light snoring (from Cat, who fell asleep after a half hour of chit-chatting), and the fact you could talk all night if you felt like it.

* * *

The very next day, Jamie went to the office, and requested to switch her dorm room.

She packed her things in boxes, and then walked to Cat's and Rosie's room. Next, she had to move her bed and bookcase and her couch. She could get her bookcase through the halls simply enough if she levitated it a few feet off the ground and turned it on its side.

But no amount of floating, or turning made the couch and bed fit through the halls. So she requested some help.

It took Jamie about five minutes to find Emily. Her group was standing around her, raving about her new dark pink streaks in her hair, while she looked at her phone.

"Hello Emily, I love your new hair, where did you get it done?" She put on her brightest grin.

"What do you want, freak?" said Emily, swiping on her phone. (She was from the very early two thousands, and technology in the slightly later two thousands interested her so much that she spent almost all her time using the witch internet and witch social media.)

"Well, I was moving to my new room, and I thought you could give me some transporting tips."

"Um, are you really that dumb? We don't learn transportation for, like, seven years," said Emily, rolling her eyes.

"Well, for the record, from what I saw on Instagram, you learned transporting from your older sister, Xena, before she went away to work in the potions business," Jamie said.

Emily's eyes widened. "Yes, I did, and I can, like, definitely help you, sure. Like, quickly though." Her voice was shaky.

Jamie smiled sweetly. "Well, then let's, like, go then." Jamie led the way, grinning. Both Jamie and Emily walked back to Jamie's old room. The bed and couch were sitting outside the door.

Emily reached to her wrist and pulled off her bracelet. She turned to Jamie. "Well, take off you're wand! Not gonna do this on my own."

"Tell me how to do it first," said Jamie.

"You float them and then you, um, picture the place it needs to go. And uh, yeah."

Jamie raised an eyebrow. "All right," she said, pointing the wand at the couch.

"Um, now close your eyes, and you'll stay like that for ten minutes."

Jamie knew what this was. Emily was going to make one of her minions take the couch to the other room. *Oh well. At least she's moving it so I don't have to.* She waited ten minutes, listening to Emily whisper-yell at some poor minion.

"Why don't we eat some lunch. Later we can go to the room." Jamie nearly fell over in shock.

"I thought you wanted things to go, 'Like, quickly' did you not?" asked Jamie, rolling her eyes.

"Jeez, wanna eat lunch or not?"

Jamie knew how this worked. Emily wanted to get into her good graces but just so she could more efficiently destroy her social status later on. But Jamie wouldn't fall for it. Not just because Emily was acting all nice.

"Sure," she said, her answer surprising her. So they walked.

III

Winter I

Cat

14

Art Class and Anna

Cat was hopeless at art. Paint, pencils, markers. She hated the fumes and she hated the teacher.

Professor Pengin was a short man, with a long handlebar mustache. The mustache badly compensated for the lack of hair on his head. The rest of his body was clad in an apron and a dark tracksuit. There was paint splattered across the whole outfit. He smelled like burnt carrots and paint thinner.

He was always complimenting people, except for Cat, who usually only got from him "Hmm, interesting."

The one thing she didn't hate about art was George. George was nice, with bright green sweeping bangs and dark navy eyes. Cat could never shake the feeling she knew him better than she did, even when someone just said his name.

Most boys were annoying. The few that weren't were already taken.

She didn't know why boys were such a valuable thing to most girls, she thought they were just like everyone else.

Boys. Strange. But...her heart always fluttered like a butterfly when George was around. Too bad there was no one to talk to about this odd butterfly effect.

She knew Jamie and Rosie were there for her. It just seemed like there were blurred lines on the boys front. Jamie never spoke about boys the way other girls did, and Rosie's musings usually ended up being about human celebrities. So Cat let the butterfly effect work its magic and kept it to herself.

Halfway through November there was a girl who walked into class. She had yellow hair, green spotted brown eyes. She wore a straw fedora, with a rainbow stripe on the brim. Her name was Anna. She didn't talk to anyone. She sat in the back and started working.

And as far as anyone knew, she never left that corner.

One day, Cat was working on her collage and pulling her hand off the paper, which had gotten stuck to it with glue, when she heard a chair scrape the ground.

Anna walked to the front of the class and handed in her project. Everyone's mouth dropped to the floor. Everyone in school had been photographed from behind. And all the colors of the peoples' hair created a beautiful rainbow Hawaiian flower.

Even Professor Pengin's face was a mix of fear, excitement and surprise at her talent. Everyone looked at Anna as she came to sit next to Cat. She swung her legs over the chair.

"What's up?"

Cat shrugged.

Anna smiled.

"So—" The door swung open. Emily and her clones walked in.

"Uh, gotta go," said Anna, as she speed-walked out of the room. Emily frowned. Some girl in the Emily group smiled at Anna as she walked by, Anna waved at her and left.

The same girl walked over to Cat, who squirmed in her seat. This was far too many people to meet in a day.

"Hey, you're Cat. Jamie is your sister, right?"

Cat just nodded.

"Well, I'm June, and the coach is making me, Jamie and Emily," she motioned behind her, "volleyball captains in the new semester. So can you let Jamie know?"

Cat opened her mouth slightly while June smiled brightly at her.

"Thanks Cat, you're a peach."

Cat smiled as June turned and walked off. June seemed nice, and Cat was happy for Jamie. But the good feeling dissolved the instant Emily appeared in front of her.

"Hi." She was wearing a smile that was half, *Hi best friend*, and half, *I'm going to eat your heart with my salad.*

"In case she didn't tell you, your slimy sister has become my enemy, and if either of you slip up, *I* might slip up and release *this*." Emily held up her phone for Cat to see. There on the screen, was a picture of Rosie and Jamie kissing. It looked like a picture taken by a security camera. Cat tried not to show her shock and dismay.

Emily smiled deviously. "No mistakes. Or this goes public."

Cat watched her walked away. Then Cat ran.

15

Jamie's Secret

C at stormed back to her room through the snow-covered forest. Her head was hot despite the fact that it was freezing outside.

Another thing that Cat hated about the art class was that it was above the rest of The Academy, so you had to fall down through the base of the forest to get back to the rest of the school and her dorm.

She slammed into the floor of the little silver room, trying not to scream. A voice said, "Cathrine Novice, 1824, undecided."

"Present."

"You may enter the—" Cat stomped in. Her boots were covered in snow and ice crystals. The floor was wet with melted snow where Jamie and Rosie had left their boots. Cat pulled off her boots and jacket.

Jamie was on the couch, her legs draped over the armrest.

"Hey, you're super red. Are you okay?" Jamie had a book in her hands. A book, Cat realized, that Rosie had given her that morning.

Cat nodded and huffed off toward her bed.

Rosie and Jamie. Jamie and Rosie. Cat hated to admit that it made sense to her, but it did. They were good together. She wasn't bothered by the fact that they were both girls. Okay, maybe a little. No, it was that neither of them had *told her.* She was Jamie's sister for god's sake!

"Um, Jamie, will you, come over here for a second?"

Jamie swung her legs back to the floor, and walked over to where Cat now sat, on the edge of her bed.

"What's up?"

Cat took a deep breath.

"So, um, Emily is determined to keep us in line."

Jamie breathed in sharply.

"What did you do to her?" Cat mentally smacked herself, that was not the question to ask.

Jamie looked angry. "She said some stuff, really mean stuff, she found out a secret about me, and I, uhh…"

Cat raised her eyebrows.

"I dumped my soup on her head."

Cat had to keep herself from laughing. "Well, she really doesn't want you to embarrass her again I guess, because she has a photo of you and Rosie…"

Jamie was a little bit paler, and beckoning her to tell more.

"…kissing."

Jamie went red.

Come on Jamie, this is your chance to not lie, this is your chance to tell me the truth, Cat wanted to scream these words at her.

Jamie looked down at her lap. When she looked up, her eyes flickered with a lie, and her face passed through shadow.

Don't lie, don't lie, please Jamie please.

"It must be photoshopped," Jamie said. "I never kissed Rosie."

Cat's face fell. "Okay then." She stood up and walked to the door.

"Where are you going?"

"Library. I need to clear my head."

"Why?"

Cat turned, pulling her sweater over her head, and grabbing her scarf off the hook. She gave Jamie a stinging look. "Why do you think?"

Jamie stared at her blankly.

"By the way," Cat added in a softer voice, as she opened the door, "you made volleyball captain."

16

The Violets Are Stranger Than Usual

As Cat walked through the door, and into the snowy twilight, someone bumped right into her. Well, three of the same person.

"Hello" "Cat" "How" "Have" "You" "Been?"

Cat mustered up a sweet smile and opened her mouth.

"Oh" "My" "Cat" "You" "Must" "Be" "Freezing" "Cold."

Cat again opened her mouth.

"We" "Wanted" "To" "Send" "Apologies" "To" "Jamie" "For" "Nearly" "Taking" "Her" "Head" "Off."

Cat smiled, and this time spoke before she could be interrupted. "Hi Violets, yes, Jamie is doing better. She's doing her classes from her dorm for the month, and she hates being inside for the winter."

"Oh" "We" "Are" "So" "Sor-" Suddenly the three Violets arms smacked their sides, and their heads snapped back, and then slowly moved down.

The purple of their irises had spread to the rest of their eyes, and now they were glowing.

Cat couldn't even open her mouth this time.

"Listen closely," said all three girls in unison. Their voices had gotten deeper, like the voice of an old man. Their bodies were glowing and their hair was floating up above them. "Cat, for years you have silenced me, with your very existence,"

Cat felt her legs shake as she reached out her hand to grab the Violets. "What do you mean—"

"SILENCE!" shrieked the girls, holding out their left hands, causing Cat to fly backwards into a snowbank.

"Cat! Listen!"

Cat's lower lip trembled.

"For a dozen years I've been reeling in the dungeons, waiting for you to come, waiting for you to free me. Go to the dungeon, free me, and I will not harm you, you will be protected from the wrath I will bring upon your peers."

Cat was shaking from cold, and snow was melting on her face, forming cold drips on her cheeks, and the salt water from her own tears was mixing with the melted snow.

The three violets held out their hands, forming a sort of circle, and their hands lit up and created a giant dark purple ball, shimmering and glowing. The ball flew into Cat's hands, then broke apart to reveal a shimmering sapphire locket on a long silver chain. Then something golden was thrown into her stomach. It hurt so much Cat couldn't even see through the white hot pain.

"That," said the three girls, "should help you find me." Suddenly their bodies shook, and a dark purple cloud came out of their mouths, and they fell to the floor in perfect unison.

The dark purple cloud flew past Cat's head and, as it passed her, a pair of bright green eyes stared right into hers.

"You have one month." Then the cloud puffed out of existence. Cat stood up, letting the locket and golden object fall clattering to the ground. She crouched over the Violets.

"Violets, are you okay?" Cat practically screamed. The Violets sat up and gazed blankly at the snow bank, then back at Cat.

"The demons will rise again," the Violets said, and sounded like themselves again, but still Cat was worried. She helped the three girls up. All three were shaky and red eyed.

"Violets, you need to get to the witch hospital *now.*"

"Thank" "You" "Cat." The girls hooked their arms through each other's. "We're" "Not" "Sure" "What" "Happened" "But" "We'll" "Get" "There" "On" "Our" "Own."

Cat gave them a concerned look and said, "Are you sure?"

They nodded, and she watched them walk away. She felt scared. The feeling of betrayal was still sitting strangely in her stomach, but it was drowned out by the fear swirling around in her head.

She'd have to do some research. But first, before catching a teacher carriage, she ran to the snow bank and picked up the locket and golden object, sticking them in her jacket pocket.

The image in her mind was her eyes, and *It's* eyes.

Those eyes were one and the same.

* * *

Cat flagged down a carriage that was from the nineteen eighties, all decked out in disco things. She knocked on the door, and the potions teacher opened it.

"Why, hello Cat! How are you and Jamie doing?"

Cat was too cold and shaky to answer, so she just stepped inside. Rude? Maybe, but she was just too upset.

"All right, not a talker, I get it."

65

Cat sat on the edge of the seat, and looked out the window of the carriage. Ms. Havlu said something, but Cat didn't hear her.

"Cat!"

Cat spun around. Ms. Havlu was yelling and making dramatic hand movements. "I can't take you anywhere if I don't know where you want to go. Now," said Ms. Havlu, brushing off her skirt, the beads on it shaking and . "Where would you like to go?"

Cat felt like she should smile, but nothing felt like it would be more fake, and so she kept her mouth in a straight line.

"Come on, just tell me, I don't bite." After a moment Ms. Havlu sighed, and Cat leaned against the window, pressing her cheek on it.

"Cat, I'm about to kick you out and make you walk."

Cat whispered, "Take me to the library."

Ms. Havlu sighed and repeated the directions.

The carriage lurched forward and then backwards, making Cat fly into the side of it and get glitter all over her face. She wiped off the sparkle, and braced herself against the shiny silver seat, holding so tight onto the locket that it left an indent in her hand.

17

Cat's Secret

C at was lying in bed, trying and failing to sleep. She had ignored Jamie all day. And now she and Rosie were asleep, and she was staring at the wall where their coats were hanging and noticing that her front pocket was glowing blue.

Cat had been trying not to care about the strange objects. *If I do not take them out of the pocket,* It *won't get me. I cannot take them out.* And yet, she wanted to take them out. *One peek can't hurt.* Cat threw off her covers, her feet practically freezing when they touched the cold floor. She pulled on a pair of thin stockings and over that a pair of warm fuzzy socks that without the layer of insulation would make her feet itch. She walked across the floor quietly, trying not to step on the one particularly creaky floorboard in the center of the room.

Cat reached into the pocket of her coat. She felt the objects shake with magic. She took them out and tiptoed back to her bed, pulling the heavy blanket over her chilled body. Kicking off her socks, she pulled the quilt over her head, the dark cocoon it formed illuminated by the blue light coming from the locket. She rolled the golden object in her palms, feeling its heaviness. Then something pricked her palm. She noticed an emerald button on the locket and clicked it, revealing a little screen that said the direction to go next was down.

Down to where?

Cat looked lower, where there was a clock counting down the hours. There seemed to be a lot of them.

730. 001 hours. It sounded like a lot, but maybe not enough. After all, how much longer could she wait for *It* to tell her where to go. Or was she going to find *It* on her own. And then what?

She ran her hand over the clock bit and felt a bump. She pressed the bump and the screen flipped open, revealing a tiny key. Cat pulled it out.

It was so quiet in the room, Cat could actually hear the buzz of the magic under the blanket. She dropped the key on the mattress and picked up the locket. It glowed in her palm as she tried to pry it open.

Unable to open it, she looked at the tiny key. *Aha!* There was a small keyhole in the back of the locket. The key fit perfectly. She turned it.

Suddenly, the whole room lit up with the bright blue light. Then the light died down, and now the glow was faint enough that she could see a small gem inside, a bright blue stone, the source of the light. She decided this little gem was important, and she clasped the necklace around her neck.

She looked at the golden circle, running her pointer finger over the smooth crevasses.

She opened the clock and the screen flashed at her, and it showed a little picture of The Academy and then the picture zoomed into Cat's dormitory building. A small blue light covered one of the windows.

In a bright blue scrawl across the scene were the words, **You are**

here. Then it zoomed up and then down into the ground. In a bright red scrawl it showed the words, **You need to be here. Soon.** Cat took a deep breath and closed the golden clock. The dark red sparkling dot was over the door to the dungeon.

* * *

Welcome back Cat,
  I'll be back
  While you search
  Here we are.
  It. Cat frowned.
  I have a name Cat.
  A name and a face.

In the middle of the forest, the dark purple shimmering cloud glowed and shot into the sky and a man with pasty white skin and floaty purple hair was thrown to the ground in *Its* place.

He was smiling slyly, and his bright green eyes squinted at Cat like he was amused by her. She felt confused. Because he looked just like Jamie.

"Hello Cat. I'm Lincha."

If Jamie had been male and had short purple hair and was maybe twenty years older, they'd look exactly the same. Cat was staggered as she saw a crooked canine tooth when he smiled. She instinctively ran her tongue over the same one in her mouth.

"You're my father."

His grin dimmed slightly. "Yes, I wondered when you would figure that out."

"Why do you hate us then?" Cat shook, aware she must look angry. Her lip quivered slightly, her porcelain skin turned bright red.

"All first born children of demons grow up to kill their parents. That's just how it is."

Cat was dumbstruck.

Cat watched him pace the forest floor. "Why isn't Jamie here? She's older and more likely to kill a person anyway. If you're issuing this dream to torture us, you might want her here right?"

Lincha smirked and leaned against the tree. "You make a good point. If I were more paternal I'd be proud of your vocabulary. But I'm not here to torture you, Cat. I'm here to tell you what to do. To find me."

Cat bit her lip. "But why me? I'm not good at finding things, and I'm not brave." She twirled a lock of hair around her finger.

"Hmm," Lincha mused. "Now, why would I choose the younger girl who isn't going to kill me, who has less to lose if she goes down, who hates to lie, and who if she told anyone they wouldn't believe her anyway? And who also, by the way, is more talented at magic?"

Cat saw his point. She had been more proficient at magic from beginning.

"But why won't anyone believe me?"

He smirked and yawned. "Oh my dear daughter…"

Cat cringed.

"I think your teachers will choose not to tell you they believe your words."

"What if I don't let you be free?"

His face darkened slightly and he walked close to her. She could feel his breath on her face. "Then I will free myself eventually, and when I find you, I will grind your bones to dust. I will be soaked in your and your sister's blood, and I. Will. Be. Happy." He stepped back.

Cat was visibly shaking. "How do I know you wouldn't do that anyway if *I* let you free?"

"You don't," he said, shrugging. "But there is a better chance you won't get pulverized into a puddle of Cat juice if you do. And while I can't say the same for your sister—because she can't be alive to kill me—I can at least say that for you."

"But how will you kill her? If she's destined to kill you—"

"Someone will kill her for me. Anyway. Instructions will be left around The Academy, and at the end, you'll know the time and the place that you'll find the secret entrance and then you're good to go."

Cat was horrified. She tried not to show it, tried not to let him see how scared she was . Instead of crying, she let loose a bloodcurdling scream. She screamed and couldn't stop, until her throat was all dry and rough, and she didn't even care. She screamed and kicked his knees in—well, *tried* to kick his knees in. But all she got when she connected with his leg was pure cloud, her foot went right through him and hit the tree behind him.

He smirked. "Goodbye, Cat."

Her eyes flew open suddenly. Jamie was sitting on the end of her bed. Cat tried to pretend she was still asleep, but she wasn't fooling anyone.

"Hey, you okay?" said Jamie.

"I'm fine." She pulled the blanket back over herself even though she was drenched with sweat. She wanted to stay there forever, but she knew she was running out of time.

18

The Ides Of December

"Ugh." Cat turned over on her side to face a plaid-clad torso. Rosie chuckled and patted Cat on the head, saying, "You look like a tired raccoon."

Cat smacked her leg, and Rosie snatched Cat's hands and pulled her up.

"Come on, Cat! It's a good day. They always make cool announcements on the ides of December!"

Cat felt like she'd fallen asleep on a bed of nails, so she couldn't possibly care about announcements.

As she climbed out of bed, she felt the flood of nightmares come back. She went to the closet on shaky legs, pulling out a checked pink and white dress. She pulled it on, then went to the sink and threw water on her face.

Jamie was dressed so warmly she looked like a bundle of clothes with eyes. Cat put on her long purple peacoat and her stripey scarf, then bent over to pull on her leather boots over her thick socks. She felt like a zombie. The girls walked to the dining hall.

At the drink counter, Rosie and Jamie got cups of juice, and Cat made herself a mug of tea with milk and sugar (*a lot* of milk and sugar). She took a huge sip and felt slightly better.

Everyone was running around because it was chocolate chip and blueberry pancake day. The three girls all helped themselves to a stack of pancakes, then found a table. Cat drowned her pancakes in syrup and spooned fruit onto it.

There were three things churning her stomach.

1. The secrets she was keeping.

2. The fear of having a dangerous task with deadly consequences.

3. A stack of pancakes drowning in syrup and fruit.

After breakfast, Cat and Jamie bade goodbye to Rosie, then walked to their mailboxes on the far side of the hall. Rosie walked to hers on a different side.

Inside their boxes were tickets for the Winter Dance.

Cat held the invite in her hand, and thought to herself, *Where will I get a floor-length dress?* But floor length dresses were the least of Cat's problems.

She was about to go to *Finding your element 101* and suddenly saw a small piece of dark purple paper folded six ways, with shimmery letters spelling *Cat*, in the very back of the mailbox. Without reading it, Cat put the note in her jacket pocket, feeling her heart jump when her hand touched the golden clock that was still there.

19

Found Your Element 101

Everyone was scrambling for a partner, just like every day. Jamie was waiting for Cat by the door, but she brushed past her sister and walked up to a girl sitting at her desk, looking sad, with her head lowered, her shoulder length yellow hair covering her face like a curtain.

"Hello, do you want to—" the girl tucked her hair behind her ear.

"Oh!" said Cat, smiling. "Hi Anna."

Anna's face lit up a bit, and she stood. "Hey! Wanna be my partner?"

Cat nodded, and they walked out onto the floor. An empty bucket, a pot of dirt and a pile of sticks. Professor Oy gave them a vague a set of instructions.

"All right class, now you vill start fire, then heat vater, cool vater, zen use vater to grow plant."

Anna smiled and stuck her hands in her pockets. "So where's your sister?" she asked, shuffling her feet while Cat set everything up.

Cat's grin dimmed. "We're just not right now."

Anna raised an eyebrow, and said, "What the what?"

"It means we're ready to fight," said Cat. They had a pleasant conversation while preparing everything, and Cat learned everything she could possibly want to know about Anna.

Anna was intelligent. She was from the nineteen sixties when being odd, artsy, and excitable was encouraged. Anna was all those things. For her whole life, her strangeness, her love of nature and animals had always made her different, and no one had ever commented on it.

Then she'd met June. On the outside June was her opposite, levelheaded, popular and cool. But the two both loved animals, art and color. They bonded, and suddenly they were best friends, and yet, June and Anna were still apart, because Emily hated Anna, for god knows what reason. But there was one class where they were together, and it was this one. While Jamie was out and Cat was preoccupied, June found her element. Time.

And suddenly Anna was alone. So she was ecstatic that Cat and her normal partner were on the outs. (Well, for the sole reason that she now had a partner she genuinely liked.)

So Cat and Anna began. Anna began the way she began every plant class. By talking to the seedling.

"Hey buddy!" Cat looked at Anna like she was absolutely crazy. Anna began humming a lullaby to the sprout, angling the pot towards the sun rays coming from the window while she hummed. Cat swore she could see flowers, sunshine, and rainbows creating an aura around her.

Cat managed a few sparks, and set the sticks on fire (a small fire, but a fire nonetheless). Then the water. She was never the one in charge of water, that was always Jamie's job.

She placed her hands on each side of the bucket and started thinking about herself filling it. Suddenly, it began to overflow, and everyone was looking at her. A scream escaped her along with the thought HALT! Then all the water flew up off the floor and formed into an enormous swirling water ball overhead.

Disband! Cat thought. And the giant water ball exploded all over the room. An evil thought came to her. *Direct the splash at Jamie!* Suddenly, the water screeched to a halt, switching directions and flying at Jamie. Cat realized it was also going to hit the professor. Jamie and Professor Oy held up their hands to block the water. But before it hit them, Cat changed her mind. *Ice!* she screamed in her mind, *Ice!* The water screeched to a halt, freezing solid and shattering to pieces, forming a shimmering rainbow of bright ice shards. Everyone screamed. Cat yelled out loud, "Steam!"

And the ice became steam. Four or five people had their hair frizz out with the humidity. Cat felt her cheeks warm with the brand new heat and with embarrassment. She raised her hands to cover her face. Professor Oy took a second to look at her hands.

The classroom was an absolute mess. The room puddled, water dripping down the walls, maps and paper posters and lists and schedules all wet and wrinkled from the steam. Worse, the paint on the walls had liquefied and was dripping a bit. Professor Oy waved a hand and said, "Class dismissed." Cat started to walk out the door, but Professor Oy stopped her.

He rubbed his temples, pulling out a bottle of golden liquid from a desk drawer and taking a huge gulp. He drummed his fingers on the desktop and adjusted his eye scarf. He held out the bottle to Cat. "Want some?"

Cat shook her head and pushed the bottle away, disgusted.

He pressed a little button on the table. It was only then that Cat noticed the five buttons, one dark blue, one orange-red, one white, one green, and one purple.

Suddenly a little trap door in the celling opened and some slightly deflated balloons and some dark blue pieces of rectangle-shaped paper fell out.

Cat opened her mouth to say something, but Professor Oy flashed her a strained smile that made him look insane. Cat stumbled backward, tripping over a deflated balloon and landing on the floor.

Professor Oy pulled his bracelet off his wrist, then he held his wand to her hand. It was only then she noticed her hands were glowing a dark blue.

Cat, still sprawled on the floor, held out her hand. Professor Oy placed the wand on her hand and performed a spell. Suddenly there was a little shield shape on her palm with an image of a waterfall over an ocean of shining rainbow waves.

"Cathrine Novice," he said, "I now pronounce you a water witch."

She had been so mesmerized by her hand that she had forgotten Professor Oy was even there, and his words snapped her back to reality.

"Thank you," Cat said, getting to her feet. She walked out of the classroom and stuck her hand in her pocket, remembering the note. She opened it, and as she read the first words felt her heart sink.

Hello Cat,

 Now, I do not wish to add a workload, so I'll keep it simple. There is a book in the headmistress's office that will let you communicate with me, without my having to leave these silly notes in your box.

 Plus, it'll give you much better guidance for your task. Steal it.

Cat felt her stomach flip flop as her eyes scanned the rest of the paper.

 And by the way,

Cat felt her heart jump.

Congratulations on finding your element.

20

Stealing from Hilda

C at went to the headmistress's office during lunch, heart pounding.

You can do it, Cat. You have to do it.

Cat raised her hand to knock on the door.

Do it Cat.

Cat hit the side of her head. *Get out of my head!*

Not till you get the book, Cat, not till you get the book.

Cat sighed and knocked on the door. She took a deep breath as the shadow of the Headmistress approached the door.

"Well hello Cat, to what do I owe the pleasure of your company?" asked Hilda, smiling brightly. *Not what,* thought Cat, *who.* "Well, come in, come in."

"So," said Hilda, smoothing down the fur collar of her green velvet coat. She caught Cat staring, and said, "I was just on my way out. So this should be quick." Cat twiddled her thumbs.

"Um, so I am not supposed to go to the library for the next week," *Lie.* "And I need a book for class," *True.* "About… Dragons." *Where did that come from?* And then Cat frowned because she knew exactly where it came from. *Lincha.*

Headmistress Hilda's face lit up. "Oh my! I have so many recommendations for you! Give me five minutes." She floated into the back of her office, and poked her head out quickly. "Be right back!" The door shut behind her.

What did you do? **Nothing, just gave her- excuse me, you gave her a push in the right direction.** *Why dragons?* **She and I always talked about dragons.** *Wait, you knew her?* **Yes, back to the plan.** *So, what now?* **There's a book on the shelf, it's dark purple, gold lettering, it's got my name on it.** *So I just take it?* *It seems like she'd miss it.* **She will. That's why you're going to make an exact copy, without the magic in it.** *Why does she even have that book?* **Not important.** *But-* **Do it Cat!** *FINE.* **Is that any way to talk to your father-** *Shut up!* **Did Jamie teach you that foul language? Now get the job done.**

Cat walked up to the book shelf, and reached out. Suddenly she had the idea she should use the hand that didn't have the mark on it, so as not to get the books wet. So she pulled out the book Lincha had specified and pressed her hand to it.

Suddenly a second book appeared in her hands but this one didn't hum with magic. **Good job, Cat.** *Get out of my head.* **Not until you get away with it.** She sighed and put the book behind her back as Hilda came flying in with a stack of books bigger than Cat.

Hilda ducked down behind the desk, and this gave Cat the opportunity to stick the book into the stack. **What on earth are you doing?** *Just trust me.* She took a random book from the pile, and then she pulled out Lincha's book, and held them both to her chest.

Hilda smiled, and Cat managed a watery grin, but then she stepped backwards and stumbled out the door, and said as fast as she could, "Um, thankyouheadmistresshildagottogoI'mquitethankfulforthese-booksaboutdragonsformypotionsclassprojectgoodbye!" And she slammed the door behind her.

Well done, Cat. Well done. *Get out of my head now.* **As promised.** Cat felt her head spin and saw a tiny little purple cloud fly away.

She sighed, and turned the corner. She slumped against the wall. Cat started to open the book, and suddenly there was a loud croaking sound, and then Cat realized the bell was ringing for the end of lunch.

She was starving. And yet. She hid the book in her tiny velvet purse. She cracked opened the dragon book, and then started reading, hiding behind the book, feeling raw and angry, and feeling tears well up in her green eyes, which suddenly felt a little less beautiful, and a little more scary.

Sometimes she wondered about her older sister. How would she act in this situation? Did she even love them? Did she feel the emptiness by their absence that Cat felt by hers? Did she care?

Was Lincha her father?

There was a croaking sound again and Cat dashed off to Potions.

* * *

When Cat got to Potions almost no one was there, not even Ms. Havlu, so she was basically alone in the bright lights and quiet. She slipped the dragon book back into the little purse and pulled out the other book and opened it up.

Inside were what seemed like maybe two hundred pages of field notes about…something. Some was in English, some was in Latin, some was in a language she didn't know. She figured out from reading the neat scrawl on the front page that the field notes were taken in "The forest of demons" and the dungeon, which was referred to as "the holding place for demons." And the pages were just paragraphs of notes, but there were also little diagrams, and drawings of demons, both in cloud and human form.

She flipped through, barely skimming the pages, until she got to the end. Then she found letters. Letters written in two different hands.

She started to read the first letter, but suddenly Jamie slid into the seat next to her, and Cat slammed the book shut.

"Hey, what's up—"

Cat got up and moved to another desk. Jamie frowned at her. She started to get up to follow, but June sat on the desk and started talking to her. Jamie looked like she was listening intently. Cat felt a little bad about brushing her off, but she knew that if she'd said even a quick "Hello" everything would spill. (And she was mad at Jamie for the Rosie-kiss-lying thing.)

June slipped off the table and sat in the seat Cat had been in before, and Jamie and she struck up a conversation, laughing and talking like best friends. This left Cat, as Rosie might have put it, "Confuzzled." On the one hand, she was really happy Jamie had a different friend, since *she* wasn't talking to her; on the other, she wanted to turn June into a giant fiery ball of lava and watch her burn to a crisp. Jamie was *her* best friend, not June's, and didn't June already have a best friend? At least she wasn't the only one who was upset about this new friendship.

Anna had walked in holding a bottle of potion, and she looked at the two girls like she had seen a ghost. Cat glanced again at the two girls, and noticed that they were doing some kind of handshake, and Jamie was laughing in a way Cat had never seen.

Anna seemed horrified by this display, tears running down her face like little waterfalls. Then her homework slipped out of her hand and smashed to smithereens on the ground.

Everyone within a few feet of her got sprayed by a strange green liquid that caused splotchy purple rashes where it hit them.

Anna waved her wand and the damage undid itself, and she promptly ran out of the room, leaving Cat and everyone else staring and feeling very confused.

June got up in the confusion and made a face like she'd realized what she'd done, and then ran out the door after her friend.

Cat slumped down in her seat. Just then Ms. Havlu burst through the doors.

"Goodness, " Ms. Havlu said, "well, you all look like you're having the most boring time waiting for me, so, I'll begin."

21

Midterms

Somehow Cat and Jamie had gone five whole days without speaking, and it seemed like they might make it to Christmas without a word between them. Rosie had been lighting her menorah all week, and she was on her final days. Everyone was preparing for the winter dance, and Cat found it slightly annoying.

Cat *had* been worried about the dance, thinking she had nothing to wear, but it felt less important than figuring out the secrets of Lincha's book.

Cat, Jamie, and Rosie went on a dress search through the witch internet, looking for floor-length dresses.

Rosie found a floor-length lavender gown, with little lilacs in a pattern around the skirt. And then Jamie found a dress with thin sparkling lace over a bright green dress with a purple shining sash around the gown.

But Cat couldn't find anything. Nothing interested her, and honestly, she didn't care. She needed time for research, so she wasn't going. And that was that.

The halls had tinsel and pine branches all over them, and there were huge Christmas trees in the dining halls.

They were decorated with candles, lit with little dots of colored light, and glass balls, with little winter scenes inside, and some pieces of glass fruit.

The whole dining hall was lit up like a star, but Cat was too distressed to care. The world was bright and shining, and yet, in Cat's brain, the world was dark, scary, and full of the fact that she still didn't know squat about Lincha's book. There were letters, between him and, an *H.A.* Who on earth was *H.A?* And why were she and Lincha writing letters to each other? And why were they in this book? Cat had studied the field notes over and over, but nothing made sense. It seemed like nothing was making sense these days. When Rosie and Jamie got their dresses one day, Cat was scanning a few sketches of Lincha. She was puzzled by these, but she kept it to herself.

Just like she was keeping everything to herself.

On the day that the dresses arrived, Jamie and Rosie were trying on their new gowns and asking Cat's opinion.

They both looked beautiful, and Cat couldn't be bothered to care.

* * *

Cat was yawning her way through another art class later that day, when a loud croaking sound filled the room. Headmistress Hilda's voice came over the speakers in each room. She said;

"Cathrine Novice, Jamison Novice, and Rosalina Porter, please report to my office to take your midterm exam!" Cat felt her heart stop for a moment when she heard her name, thinking Headmistress Hilda had caught her with the book.

But she'd forgotten all about midterm exams. She made her way to the coat rack, took off her coat, and headed out the door.

Jamie and Rosie were already in Headmistress Hilda's office. Headmistress Hilda wasn't saying anything, just flipping through papers on her desk. She stood up abruptly, holding three pieces of paper, and nodded for the girls to follow her as she started out of the office. The girls glanced at one another briefly then followed her. Hilda led them all the way up to the forest of golden trees, at which point she stopped and handed them a paper, giving them no instructions except, "Good, luck." Then, waving her wand, she created a purple gap in the air, and stepped through it like it was nothing. Someone needed to teach Cat how to do that.

Cat opened the square of paper in her hand. Her two comrades did the same, unfolding the note and reading it carefully.

> *Girls,*
>
> *Hello and welcome to your midterm exam. In four and a half minutes, I will release a creature of pure evil. You will have two hours to travel across time to find it. You each have a task.*
>
> *~Rosie, yours will be mapping and trying to navigate time and land.*
>
> *~Jamie, yours will be using your motor skills to get each vehicle around and chase the demon down.*
>
> *~Cat, you must use logic and magic to catch the demon in the easiest way you can. If you fail, I will come there and help you.*
>
> *Good Luck.*
>
> *Headmistress*

Cat sucked in a deep breath. It was then that Jamie pointed out the sleek black car behind the nearby stand of trees. Jamie's face lit up like it was Christmas, and she ran over.

"Omygosh! I totally can hot-wire this baby!"

Rosie looked shaken.

Cat made a face as she read the last line.

"Oh," Cat breathed quietly, "we will need it."

22

Demon Chase

Rosie strangely did not request the front seat, so Cat slid in next to Jamie. Suddenly the forest floor opened a few feet away and something came flying out. It was like Lincha in cloud form, except green. It started to fly away, heading for a small portal. Cat and Jamie both caught their breath, but Cat kept her gaze steely and straight ahead, refusing to engage Jamie's imploring glances.

Frustrated, Jamie looked back at Rosie. Rosie nodded, then pulled out her wand. She pointed at the navigational system.

"Follow that demon, throughout time and land, do whatever you must, or make any changes in your form to blend in." The navigational system beeped for a moment, and then exploded. Rosie slumped back into her seat, rubbing the space between her eyes. "Fine. Let's just run around trying to find that thing," Jamie nodded.

Jamie had spent about four minutes "hot-wiring" the car (which

Rosie called a Cadillac) but now all that seemed to be forgotten. She stepped on a pedal under the wheel (she had to basically fall to the floor to do this) and the car lurched forward. With the car speeding along, Rosie looked extremely sick. Cat couldn't say she blamed her.

The tires screamed as they sped around the clearing. Rosie looked very green. She held out her wand and pointed it where the demon had disappeared. Suddenly a little rip in the sky appeared.

The car was sucked through it. Cat felt absolutely sick. Rosie made a loud retching sound. Jamie slammed the brake with all her might. They landed, realizing they were inside a sort of, well the only way Cat could describe it would be a hippie van. Rosie defogged the window nearest to her face, and even though she still looked green, she said in quite a steady voice,

"Fasten your seatbelts. We're gonna do that a few more times."

Cat swallowed. Jamie sped them through the roads after the demon, and then through the rip in the air. Cat held her seatbelt tightly.

"Jamie?" asked Rosie after they landed in a huge clunker van somewhere in the eighties. She tapped Jamie on the shoulder and Jamie turned around. "Yeah?"

"Can you pull over, I think I'm gonna be sick."

"No! We are not stopping! Just try not to barf, and open the next portal time rip thing please."

Cat turned around and asked, "What on earth is *barf*?"

Before Rosie could answer, the car plunged down into the ground. Suddenly Cat and Jamie were sitting on the front seat of an old wooden wagon, and Rosie was spayed out in the open cart of hay behind them. A donkey was pulling the wagon—or at least had been.

The donkey stood there, as if waiting for instructions. Jamie kicked it and yanked the reins. The donkey did not move.

"Oh for Pete's sake." Cat reached over and grabbed the reins and yanked, and then, when the donkey still didn't move, sighed with annoyance, as the demon flew away and into a tiny green speck.

"Move, Stupid," Cat mumbled. She whipped the rein on the donkey's long neck. The donkey began to move at last and Cat handed the reins back to Jamie.

Rosie pointed her wand at the place in the sky where the demon had disappeared, and the cart got sucked up into the portal. This time, Cat opened her eyes. And the cart splintered around the girls. Pieces of a futuristic silver and blue car pieced together around them.

When they landed, they hadn't actually landed. They were in some kind of hover-car, and the demon was flying around very close by.

"Yeah baby!" screamed Jamie as she slid down to press the gas. The demon seemed to notice them and flew away fast, but Jamie made sure they weren't far behind. With the sudden speed, Rosie was slammed very, very, very hard into her seat. She retched, and let out a slight whimper.

"Jamie?"

"Rosie-"

"I really am going to be sick—"

"Does it look like I care?"

"But—"

"ROSIE! I AM NOT STOPPING THIS CAR, SO SHUT UP, AND OPEN THE NEXT RIP, THANK YOU VERY MUCH!" Jamie's face was an alarming shade of red. Rosie shrank back in her seat. She held up her wand.

This time they landed in a large stone box with windows. "Um, what the heck?" Jamie hit the stone wall.

This was the first time Cat noticed that as they traveled, their clothes were changing as well as the vehicle. Now she was wearing some kind of animal skin and no shoes.

"I do believe, we're in caveman times." These were the first words she had uttered since the incident with the donkey.

"Well do *you* have any suggestions on how to make us move?"

Jamie was still fire engine red. She seemed even angrier than before.

Suddenly a very hairy caveman stuck his face in one of the "windows" and made a strange noise, a cross between a gurgle and a bark. Jamie was so angry and upset that she turned around and, pulling her arm back, gave him a swift punch in the face. Suddenly, even though no one had noticed, the rip pulled them in, and Rosie made her retching sound again.

* * *

A few more time jumps and the girls were in a fancy looking carriage pulled by a horse. Sometime earlier, it had seemed to Cat that Rosie needed to go to the bathroom quite badly, although she was trying not to say anything (she'd seen what had happened to that caveman).

Jamie squinted to find the demon, and then Rosie opened the next rip. They landed in a... tank?

That was what Jamie called it anyway. It was some kind of war thing...that did something. Cat realized she was dressed in a dirty, slightly bloodstained camouflage army suit, and she was standing, with bullets pounding the sides of the tank and Rosie curled up in the corner, shaking and mumbling in Russian, and Jamie nowhere to be seen.

Cat was beginning to freak out a little bit. Was that Jamie screaming for her? Cat made her way up a small metal ladder.

She peeked over the top rung, and there was Jamie. She whispered hoarsely, "We're in World War Two."

The world went to war with each other twice? That is absolutely terrible.

"Wait, Jamie, there!" In the middle of the battle field, with bullets flying around, floated the bright green demon. Cat pointed her wand right at it. An enormous glass bubble formed, capturing it. Just like that the task was done.

23

The Aftermath of the Demon Chase

"Well, that was easy," said Jamie a few moments later (or a few years later depending on your point of view).

The two other girls glared at her.

"Oh come on, it's a *joke*!" said Jamie. When both girls continued to glare, she sank back in her seat.

"Why do you think it was just floating there?" mused Rosie from the back seat, where she was lying down, her legs twisted like licorice whips.

"I can actually answer that," Cat said. Since demons are made of pure evil and chaos, and when we were there was so much chaos and evil, the demon felt very upset, a sort of demon depression." She'd been doing some research.

Rosie snorted. But then thought again and covered her mouth.

When the girls got back to the forest of golden trees, they scrambled out of the car, and sat on the forest floor. Rosie looked like she would burst.

After waiting for several moments, Rosie stood up, and said, "Well, the Headmistress seems not to be here, so I'm gonna split."

"Um, no! You can't leave!" said Jamie in a panic.

Rosie ignored her, heading off toward the trees. But then, to Jamie's relief, she seemed to change her mind and turned, beckoning them to follow her. So they did, walking in silence, waiting for instructions, until the forest floor suddenly opened up, and the three girls and the trapped demon fell through. The girls landed with a hard thud and found themselves standing on shaky feet in the headmistress's office.

The Headmistress looked up from her papers, and the girls handed over the orb holding the demon. Headmistress Hilda looked impressed.

"Well done, girls! I can't believe what you accomplished in such a short amount of time." Hilda continued to talk about talent and danger and this and that, and Cat was feeling very tired, and when would this be over, and…

"Cat! Are you paying attention?"

Cat, who had definitely *not* been paying attention, nearly jumped. She swallowed and said, "Sorry Headmistress. I just got a little head in the clouds-ee."

The Headmistress took off her reading glasses and rubbed the bridge of her nose. Then she waved the girls away. "Just leave. Congratulations, you passed your midterm girls."

Cat tried not to cry. She tried not to cry when they got back. And when she found a letter to *her* in the back of the book, and when she dressed again, and when she read it.

But when she got into bed, she stopped trying not to cry and let the tears run free. And she read the letter again.

Dear Cat,

Hello and salutations! Just so you know, you can write, and I'll write back. I have some updates! You must go to that dance. An event like this is the perfect cover for dungeon infiltration! Excellent no? Please go,

I've figured out that Rosie has bought you a gown already.

Merry Christmas, Cathrine!

Love Lincha

The "love" made Cat's eyes water again, but she held herself together and pulled out a pen and began to write back. The pen is mightier than the sword.

Dear Lincha

Thank you for the instructions, I'll attend the dance, and I'd like you to do one thing for me.

Please do not hurt me or Rosie or anyone in this school. Please, I need people to stay alive. I just don't want people to die from my actions. I read about the "ever binding promise." Please make one. I need no one from this school to die.

Cat

Cat took a deep breath, *Worth a shot,* she thought, closing the book, and placed it on her dresser and felt her eyes water again.

24

Christmas Day

As the snow shivered down outside, Cat opened her eyes. The sky was gray and cloudy, and she was up at 6:30 in the morning like a child, but whatever. She looked over at the tree they'd put up the day before and noticed the small cluster of presents under it.

Rosie had agreed begrudgingly to celebrate Christmas with them, along with Hanukkah, but saving presents from her parents to the twins for Christmas. Cat saw the boxes she not-so-stealthily-hid under the tree the night before.

Unfortunately, she had made the Christmas presents for Jamie and Rosie before she was mad at Jamie, so Jamie had a handmade doll that looked just like her, a candy cane, and an orange in her stocking.

She saw her slightly bulging stocking, and smiled against her will. But she knew that tomorrow she'd have to not only engage in a socially awkward party, but release her father, a demon, from the dungeon of the school.

She touched the locket, tracing her finger along the gem on the front.

Her chest tightened again, and she suddenly was feeling a little less happy, and she tried to go back to sleep.

About ten minutes later, Rosie was shaking her awake and screaming, "OmigodCatIt'sChristmas!"

She jumped up and down and smiled brightly. Then she leaned close and whispered, "Am I Christmas-morning-ing? I know this is what they do in movies."

Cat grinned. "You're fine." The lavender girl pulled her best friend out of her fluffy covers.

Jamie was already sitting down on the floor, holding a mug of that hot brown stuff, and she smiled.

"Merry Christmas, sis." Cat couldn't help but smile back. *Oh come on, Cat, it's Christmas.* So she sat down next to her sister, and swung her arm over Jamie's shoulders and basically knocked their heads together.

"Merry Christmas." Cat felt her sister's shoulders slump and lean closer to her. The girls both smiled.

"Yay!" yelled Rosie, jumping up and down. "Sister-bestie status quo restored!" Jamie smiled. Cat felt hers slip.

No, I'm not ready to forgive you yet, Jamie. She removed her arm and moved away.

"Or not," whispered Rosie. Jamie looked crestfallen. Cat picked up a mug.

After the girls had each drunk half their cocoa, and eaten a Christmas muffin Rosie had made, they decided to dig into the gifts. There was barely a discussion before the girls were ripping open packages.

"Rosie?" asked Cat about ten minutes into their ripping spree.

"Hmm?" responded Rosie, her mouth full of candy cane.

"Your grandparents are so kind to give us presents considering they've never met us… but what are these?"

"Gelt," said Rosie, pointing to the gold foil covered chocolate coins, smiling and unwrapping one, and throwing it directly into Cat's open mouth. Cat felt a cool cocoa taste flood her mouth.

"Yum," she said, unwrapping the next gift.

A roll call of gifts:

Stocking:

Gelt: Rosie's grandparents

Cherry candy canes: Jamie

Tiny silver necklace with a C on it: Rosie

Under the tree:

Book, *Fog Magic*: Rosie's grandparents

Army hat with a black braid and silver buttons: Jamie

The most beautiful gown Cat had ever seen: Rosie.

Rosie had handed her the dress in its box. It had a satin pink bow tied neatly around it, and the box was smooth and white.

"You didn't find anything you liked, so I got you something after I did a little more looking." Rosie grinned and placed the box gently in Cat's arms.

"Happy Hanumas." Then she went to sit with Jamie. Cat pulled off the satin ribbon, and opened the top of the box.

Staring up at her was a few folds of tissue paper, and under that was something aqua and shimmery. And some kind of sapphire and pink diamond brooch. Cat whipped around to look at her friend.

"Rosie, where on earth did you get this jeweled brooch? Are those diamonds?" Rosie smiled, and responded,

"My grandparents own a jewelry store, and they got some pretty brooches from some other jeweler. I gave Jamie one as well for her dress," Cat nodded and pulled back the tissue paper.

* * *

The rest of the day was spent trying on their dresses for the hundredth time, and watching a DVD; which Cat declared was the best example of technology she'd ever seen, to which Rosie responded; "Dude, 'Elf' isn't *that* good."

It was the best Christmas Cat had ever had.

25

The Winter Dance

C at hadn't been to a dance since she was ten years old.

Her "father" had been a war hero, and he was always invited to big fancy balls, until he came down with the plague when Cat was eleven. He died, not like a hero, but like an old man, and it left a gaping hole in Cat's heart.

She never wanted to go to a dance again.

But tonight she was on a mission.

Rosie was on the planning committee, and Jamie had tagged along that afternoon, so Cat was getting ready alone.

She studied herself in the mirror.

Her long blue hair was in a neat fishtail braid, and she had combed glitter through it, so it would sparkle. She had sewn a small pocket into her shawl so she could put her little purse inside. Inside of *that*, was the locket, and the golden clock.

She lifted her skirts just slightly, to reveal her boots, and her wand, peeking out of the left boot.

The dress was incredible, the skirts were long and silky, the full skirt and jewel encrusted bodice sparkled in the slight setting sunlight.

The shawl was dark purple, and she slung it through the crooks of her elbows. She was wearing something Rosie and Jamie called "Lip Gloss" which mad her lips pink and shimmery.

She had created little wings coming out from the sides of her eyes with a dark pencil Rosie had given her, and plopped blush on the apples of her cheeks. She thought if she didn't look so sad and worried, she'd look very pretty.

She took a deep breath, and walked out the door.

* * *

Cat was slightly overwhelmed when she walked into the dining hall. The room was a burst of color and glitter and voices. Rosie, being the good eye she was, spotted her right away.

"Cat! Over here!" Rosie waved her over to where Jamie and she were standing. There was a table with snacks on it, cupcakes with multicolored frostings and a glass bowl of some kind of sparkling blue juice, and a stack of strangely patterned paper cups.

"Behold! The snack table! Where the nerds spend the dance," Rosie said.

"Aw, come on Rosie, we can be cool."

No we can't Jamie, we really can't.

"Let's dance, come on!" Jamie pulled Rosie onto the dance floor.

Cat took a huge breath in.

"Yeah, sure just forget about your sister. I'll be here." whispered Cat. She took a highly decorated cup, filled it with the sparkling blue liquid, and just stood there.

Taking a sip, she suddenly heard a voice in her ear.

"Hey Cat, good cupcakes, huh?" said the voice.

"George!" She turned to face the stranger. His bright green hair was messy and neat at the same time. His irises and pupils bled into each other in the semidarkness.

Cat's stomach did a flip-flop. She took a cupcake. It had blue cake and bright pink frosting. She took a bite, and immediately melted into the ground.

"My, they are good, aren't they."

George flashed a grin. "Told ya."

"Um, bye." She blushed and shuffled off.

As she walked to the dance floor, she ate the rest of the cupcake and tapped Jamie on the shoulder.

Jamie was dancing with a girl, who was giving her eyes like she never wanted to stop looking at her and Rosie. Jamie turned, with a dreamy look on her face, like the one in the picture of her and Rosie kissing.

"Jamie, can we talk?" Cat said.

Jamie nodded, and left Rosie dancing with Anna and June, who had made up.

"So what's up?" Jamie asked as the two walked out the door.

Cat talked quietly, and while she talked, she felt her whole body unclench in the tight dress. "Jamie, I'm not going to forgive you for lying to me, not yet, but I love you so much, and I never, ever, ever will forgive myself for what I have to do now. Goodbye." Jamie looked confused. Cat threw her arms around her sister's neck.

Jamie hugged her back, then headed inside.

"And Jamie..."

Jamie turned around to look at her pale, beautiful, glittering, sad sister. "Don't follow me."

Cat stayed there, waiting until she saw felt the little golden clock shake her purse. She pulled it out, and looked at the map. She pulled her wand out of her boot, and slapped it on her wrist.

She felt tears well up as she left, and as she looked back, her heart fell to her toes, and her mind turned to the stars.

IV

Winter II

Jamie

26

Something's Not Right

J amie knew something was not right as soon as Cat arrived at the dance.

Well, she'd known that something wasn't right when her nightmares stopped, but her sister still woke up reeling, screaming, crying, angry. But that was minor. She knew things had really gone awry when Cat stole a book from the Headmistress.

She'd known that Cat had some kind of guilt festering in her when she walked into potions class that day, but when she herself took a fast peek at the book her sister had been obsessed with for a few days, it belonged to H.A. Hilda Anborth. If the Headmistress had used her real name, it was probably a thing she didn't want students looking at. Cat was a straight edge, she'd never ever steal from anyone. And she hated that they were fighting, but Cat was determined to keep them not talking. Until five seconds ago, Jamie wasn't even sure why they were fighting, but now she wanted to make up with her, more than anything. She technically hadn't lied to Cat about the kiss. They barely touched lips! Not the big reveal Cat made it out to be. She had to admit, knowing that Emily knew gave her a stirring fear in the pit of her stomach but Cat knowing made it real. Cat was her everything, her perfect. Her normal.

So Jamie knew that Cat had something planned. She went around from the day of their midterm onward, murmuring the name, *Lincha*, and repeating the date,

December twenty sixth, December twenty sixth. Cat wasn't exactly the stealth master she thought she was.

Therefore, Jamie knew three things:

1. Cat had a secret plan, that would be carried out on the twenty sixth of December, probably while everyone was distracted with the dance.

2. The plan had something to do with someone named "Lincha" which was supposedly a boy Cat knew.

3. The book Cat stole from Headmistress Hilda was going to help, and the book was very important to the plan.

Most of this (well the first part at least) was confirmed when Cat walked out of the dance, but it added two other pieces to the puzzle.

4. If the plan succeeded Jamie and a lot of other people would get hurt.

5. Cat was not happy about being involved in the plan.

Jamie knew what Cat had told her. She shouldn't follow. But suddenly she felt a pull in her chest. Against her better judgement, she went after her sister.

Cat went back to the dorm first, and Jamie climbed up above the door frame as Cat stirred things in the room. Thank God Cat didn't turn around as she walked out and down the hall.

Cat went as far down the hallway as you could go and then down as many stairs with Jamie trailing. Suddenly the lighting got darker. Then it cut out all together. Cat's wand lit up. *Bad idea,* Jamie thought, *bad idea, bad idea.* Jamie could see that her twin's shoulders were shaking like she was either crying or laughing.

Jamie took a literal shot in the dark and guessed crying. Her sister had arrived at a big wooden door. Jamie hid behind a column and watched Cat flip through the book and say something in a loud voice to the door.

"1812." There was a click, and Cat pulled a locket out of her purse. She opened it and a bright blue light screamed through the darkness. She pulled out something and placed it in the keyhole. The door creaked open loudly. Cat stepped in. *Go back, go back!* Jamie's brain screamed at her. But she couldn't. Jamie ran out from behind the column, and slipped through the slight crack between door and wall. She felt the door slam behind her, and the pitch black became even pitch blacker. She felt around in the dark for something to hide behind. She found a slab of rock and crouched down behind it. Cat had been feeling in the dark, and suddenly, there was a blinding flash, and a huge ball of pure light appeared in midair. The ball asked Cat a question.

"Which demon shall be released, my lady?"

Cat was breathing so deeply that Jamie could hear her lungs fill and collapse. She rustled through the pages of the book, apparently finding what she was looking for. Jamie watched in disbelief. Was her sister—her perfectly normal, intelligent sister—about to release a demon from the dungeon of the school?

"Number three forty five," she said, choking out the words. "Lincha Novice."

Jamie's whole world came to a screeching halt.

Novice.

The demon had her's and Cat's last name. What on earth could that—? *It means that the demon is related to you in some way, dummy!* Jamie swallowed. And peered out again. Was that the reason Cat was doing this? Did she want to release this demon because he\she was related to them? Or was it for other reasons? Jamie knew the only thing to do was watch.

The ball of light exploded and something appeared in place of it.

It. Jamie's breath caught in her throat. She could hear blood rushing in her ears. Why did Cat want to release *It*? She was terrified and logic seemed not to apply anymore. Suddenly *It* flashed and exploded, incongruously revealing a rather bored looking older guy.

He had floaty purple hair, and—Jamie gasped the smallest of gasps—bright green eyes like theirs. He was even missing a canine tooth.

"Evening, Cat." The next few words were mostly drowned out by the loudness of her own thoughts.

What she did hear were fragments like:

"You never responded."

And

"Meant to."

And

"Ever-binding promise."

And

"You have a deal."

And

"Thank you."

Then Cat said some words that Jamie couldn't hear, followed by a flash of bright light along with more ominous colors: murky grays and dark greens.

But through all of the dark colors—through the night without stars, through the blood red, the bomb-touched sky yellow, the ashen black—was the light bouncing off Cat's pink and blue brooch and creating a rainbow on the opposite wall.

Jamie heard a few more muffled words, but even as they were uttered, she was busy pulling her wand off her wrist, preparing to fight this demon if he so much as brushed his fingers against Cat's shoulder. Cat, for her part, was also taking out her wand. Jamie could hear the wood scraping against her twin's skin. Jamie peeked out from behind her rock slab to see Cat pointing her wand right at the shining ball. Suddenly, the ball burst into a million shards of magical green glass.

Lincha rose up from where the shattered glass lay on the ground.

Jamie had never been so terrified in her entire life. She tried not to cry, but the tiny green shards in her arm didn't help. It took everything she had not to whimper. She felt blood running down her wrist.

It was like her first dream, the pounding in her ears, aching lungs. Even though she was standing completely still, her body felt angry at her for not moving, for not doing something—anything! But she stayed rooted to her spot, unable to move.

Lincha again spoke to Cat. He reached out to hug her, but Cat pressed her wand to his throat like a sword.

"No!" This was the clearest word that Jamie had heard the whole time. She peeked out as he backed up.

"Fine, be that way."

At that moment, leaning closer so she could see, Jamie lost her balance and fell forward awkwardly.

"Well, what a pleasant surprise," said Lincha with a nasty chuckle. Cat moved with amazing speed, leaning down to take Jamie's hand and help her up. "What are you doing here?" she hissed.

It was then that Jamie realized she didn't know. It was like someone else had moved her legs to make her follow Cat down those stairs and hide behind that rock. Even to make her lose her balance and fall.

"I-I-" She looked right into her sister's eyes. "I don't know."

Cat dropped Jamie's hand and turned to face Lincha. "You." She barely breathed the word. "You did this to her! Just like with the Violets! You made her come down here! And now you're going to kill her!"

"Who me?" said Lincha. He made a fake innocent face and smirked.

"I just wanted to see both of my beautiful daughters together in one place."

And then Jamie fainted.

27

I Love You Because of What You Are

And the night had been going so well.

Jamie had walked into the dance with a big smile on her face. The dining hall was so pretty, and she was already enjoying herself. She also thought maybe, just maybe, the special night would finally make her forget the way Rosie had hurt her.

She felt beautiful, her dress was pretty, her eyes sparkled in the lights, sparkled so brightly she almost couldn't see. Which is perhaps why Jamie walked right into Coach Marvlyn's daughter; Tabitha. Literally walked into her, causing them both to go crashing to the floor.

Tab had bright orange shoulder length curls with little streaks of dark blue running through it and electric violet eyes.

She had a million dark freckles marching across her face, and about a zillion more on her legs and arms, she had pillowy lips and a crooked button nose. She had always been extra cheery and nice to Jamie.

Sometimes a bit *too* nice. If Jamie hadn't been falling so hard for Rosie, maybe she would have noticed how hard Tab was falling for her.

They lay on the floor laughing.

"Omigosh, I'm so, so sorry," said Tab, grabbing Jamie's hands and lifting her up, smiling a crooked smile and showing her white teeth.

Her hands were slightly calloused, with little cuts where they'd gotten ripped doing gymnastics. Tab looked right into Jamie's eyes.

Jamie thought that Tab had very nice eyes, prettier than her eyes.

Now that she thought about it, Tab was very pretty, even in the semidarkness. She wore a tea-length pink chiffon dress and sharp heels. She looked spectacular.

All these thoughts pinged around Jamie's head as they stood there, holding hands. Just then, Rosie bounded up behind Jamie, and said excitedly, without seeing the held hands quickly separate, "Hey, what's going on?" Noticing Tab, she added, "Oh, hey *Tab*."

If Jamie had been paying attention, she'd have noticed the icy tone Rosie's voice took on as she talked to Tab. Abruptly, she said, "Jamie, I could use your assistance at the snack table," she paused, "over there."

As Jamie obediently followed Rosie, she glanced back to look at Tab, who waved at her. She waved back.

She'd felt like was having the time of her life, and then, suddenly, her life came crashing down around her.

* * *

Cat was standing over her when she woke, and this infuriated her. Why, after all Cat had done, all she'd lied about and hid, should she be able to stand over her! It was then that Jamie realized she wasn't in the dungeon anymore. Well. She had to give Cat points for that. Still.

"You've been lying to me for months!" Jamie said, from her knees.

"You've been lying too!" Cat said.

"Um, you released a demon from the school!"

"Well you—you—you—I don't know!"

The girls raged at one another until Jamie was suddenly out of breath and less angry than she had been. In the midst of a tirade about trust (even though she was one to talk), Cat saw Jamie's expression soften and lost steam.

"Okay, confession time," Jamie said. "I'll start..." she traced lazy circles on the comforter with her short scraggly fingernails.

Cat waited, ready to hear what the apology would be.

"I like girls. I like Rosie." Jamie's breath caught in her throat. "And I didn't tell you." She choked back a sob and pressed the heels of her hands into her eyes. She knew she shouldn't do that, that it could damage her eyes, but she didn't care. "Oh Cat, I'm so sorry I pushed you away. I shouldn't have lied. I just thought, if you knew the truth about me, about how I am, about where I've been...you'd stop loving me."

Cat took Jamie's hands.

"Jamie. There is nothing—nothing—that would ever make that happen. You're my sister. It might take some time for me to get used to this, but I love you *because* of who you are." She wrapped Jamie in a hug, her braid digging into Jamie's shoulder. "I love you no matter what."

"The worst part," said Jamie, "is that she doesn't even like me back!" She wiped her eyes. "Okay, now you confess. Actually, no, explain how you saved me first. No wait—"

"Jamie. I say this with love, but shut up." Cat took a deep breath. "You already know part of the confession, you were there when it happened." Cat then explained everything while Jamie listened. Though she almost lost it several times, she mostly managed to hold back her tears.

"So, how did you get me out of the dungeon?" Jamie asked.

"Well. He ran away. I let him escape." Cat's eyes filled with tears.

"I'm Идиот, глупав човек, модел*." She paused. "That means stupid."

"How many Languages do you know?"

"Six," admitted Cat with a tiny smile.

Jamie laughed. There they were. Both teary, both laughing.

"And then I managed to levitate you back here. I know he'll be back. But he can't kill you. Or me. Or anyone at the school. Not for a whole year if we don't renew the ever-binding promise. The ever-binding promise makes sure of this. It makes it impossible to perform the task that you've promised not to do."

"But," Cat twirled her loose hair around the tip of her finger. "He can wreak unknowable havoc without being contained by anything. I say we lay low until he tries to return to the school. I know I've done a terrible thing. But I'm going to make it right."

Jamie nodded, saying, "Until then, we should do a little research, and tell Rosie what happened."

"Speaking of which," Cat said, throwing her legs over the edge of the bed,"wasn't Rosie at the dance with you?"

Jamie jumped up. "OmygoohmygodAhhhh!" she shrieked, running out the door with her sister laughing behind her.

* * *

Jamie dashed over to the dining hall. She knew she looked ridiculous: Her cute pageboy haircut was messy and unkempt, her dress was wrinkled and ripped, and her eyes were red and wild. She felt like a human being who had been turned into a bug then back to a human again. She realized that her hair, dress and eyes were the least of her problems. Well, hair and dress, anyway.

She'd not only left Rosie behind, but Tab, who, she was beginning to realize, laughed just a *little* too hard at her stories and dumb jokes. Tab really *liked* her. If Rosie hadn't been a factor, Jamie might have noticed sooner. Maybe she'd have liked her back. But Tab was notorious for her temper. Probably a good idea to step lightly.

Rosie was standing, leaning against the door frame. She did not look happy. Tab was standing in a corner popping balloons with her sharp-heeled shoes. She looked even less happy. Jamie waved, and Rosie came over, looking like she wanted to punch Jamie and hug her at the same time. With eyebrows raised, she said, "You have ten seconds...."

Jamie sucked in a breath. "I'm so sorry! Cat can explain this better, so you might want to go back to the dorm, but... I'm really sorry!"

"Fine, fine. Whatever." Rosie lowered her head and walked off. Jamie instantly felt awful. She hadn't really done anything mean—other than fainting, being forgetful, and revealing bone-crushing secrets about her parents. Oh yeah, and getting a crush on another girl.

That might've been it, that last one.

Tab, for her part, looked even angrier than Rosie. Jamie breathed in deeply and braced herself.

28

Tab Vs. Rosie Vs. Jamie Vs. Headmistress Hilda

"Jamie..." Tab said calmly—and that was the last word that fit that description. "Are you blind! Why can't you take a hint, don't you know how much I like you! And you just dump me here, without saying goodbye? Why can't you just..." She continued to yell, and Jamie continued to take it. She did nothing. Tab stopped talking, and looked her dead in the eyes and crossed her arms as if to say, "Well?"

"I'm sorry, there was a family... emergency. Cat came in to... alert me."

Tab raised one accusing orange eyebrow.

"It was serious," Jamie continued. "Like really bad. Someone ran away, and our dad is not in a great place..." Translation: "My father is a demon, my sister released him from the dungeon of the school, and he's out to kill me even though he escaped. And now almost everyone including you and me are in mortal danger."

Tab breathed in. Her eyebrow regained its proper position on her face. Angry creases smoothed out slightly.

"Does it help that I would have rather stayed here with you?" Jamie offered.

Tab let a smile slip past her steely gaze, and whispered, "A little?"

Jamie smiled wide. "I'm so sorry Tab. Can we get hot cocoa and call it a cashed-in rain check?"

Tab bit her lip. But her eyes said "Yes."

Jamie grinned and said, "See you in the new year?"

Tab smiled back feeling a small twinge of happiness. Happiness she wasn't sure she deserved.

She walked out of the dining hall, heart soaring, and began humming. Her eyes shone with excitement. She felt like she was walking on air. She saw the headmistress was stamping a letter, using the wall as a desk. Jamie bounded to her and said sweetly, "Good evening Headmistress, hello! How's your Christmas week going?" Headmistress Hilda was so startled by Jamie that her little tray of hot wax, the wax seal and a letter flew out of her hands, the hot wax raining down next to Jamie's feet. Jamie was thrown off balance but some managed to catch the letter. Headmistress Hilda bent over to pick up the seal and the now empty tray. She sighed as she muttered, "Good evening, Cat."

Jamie felt hurt. "Jamie."

Hilda raised an eyebrow. "Oh yes… Jamie. You'll excuse me." She opened the door behind them and stepped in.

"Oh headmistress, that's a—" A scream and a clang. "—broom closet." Headmistress Hilda came out dripping wet with a metal bucket on her head. Jamie choked back a laugh. Angrily, Hilda opened a portal and stepped through. It was then that Jamie realized she was still had the letter in her hand.

"Wait, Headmistress!" But it was too late.

She would just leave it in the office tomorrow and—then she saw the address on letter. Her heart stopped.

Lincha Novice

1984 127 west 12st

NY NY

Jamie was bewildered. *What the heck was going on?*

* * *

When Jamie got back to the dorm she felt like a zombie. Cat was already asleep, but Rosie was awake and reading. Seeing Jamie, she perked up. Jamie dropped the letter on Cat's beside table and sighed. She shed her dress and then was left in her tiny shorts and her tank top. It was freezing in the room, so she basically dove into her bed, leaving her dress in a heap on the ground, snuggling up into her blankets. She wanted so badly to go to sleep but Rosie had other ideas.

"Hey Jamie, Cat gave me the run down on why you left. And I forgive you because—"

Jamie sighed and sat up, suddenly wide awake. She was vaguely aware of the see-throughness of her tank top. "You *forgive me*?" She jumped up out of bed. She was easily a head taller than her petite friend, and she knew that having height on someone was an easy way to make them scared of you. It didn't happen every day that she was taller than someone.

"God Rosie, you're so, so—selfish!"

Rosie shrunk back in the face of Jamie's fury, watching her pace around back and forth in front of her. "Selfish?" asked Rosie, quivering.

"Yes! You didn't ask how I *felt* about everything that happened tonight, or think about the fact that I'm bone tired and heartbroken and maybe want to sleep before you wake me up to talk about your *forgiveness.* It's all about <u>you</u>. It's about you and the fact you can't take it that I like a girl who isn't you! You are just so... frustrating!

"All you do is tease me, holding my hand, being so nice, it's all for nothing. You told me you don't like girls, that you don't like me, and then you get mad and act jealous of a girl I like? I mean, just give me... something! Just to let me know what you really think!"

Rosie stared at her. "I thought I didn't like you that way... but seeing you with her, it made me upset. And I think I like you now and I'm so confused."

"Well, it's too late. That boat left the harbor."

"Who's being selfish now? You've never had to worry about who you are! It's not as simple for me."

"I've never had to worry about who I am?" Jamie felt as if she might explode. "How stupid are you? Let me ask you something; if you do like me, if you do like girls, or girls *and* boys, or whatever, and you told your family, would you be worried about them getting rid of you because you told them? I'm guessing no. I had to move houses every month!"

Rosie looked at Jamie open-mouthed, and now Cat was up, too, awakened by their raised voices.

"I wouldn't even open my suitcase. One time I was in a foster home for ten hours. I told the foster mom I liked girls and she sent me straight back to the agency. You've always had a net to catch you and not let you crash into the sharp rocks below. I've never had that. So don't assume what it's like to be me." Jamie stopped pacing and got back into her bed, curling up in her blankets, shutting out Rosie. Shutting out the universe.

Cat asked Jamie later if things would have gone differently if she'd noticed she was floating.

* * *

119

Jamie ran, her heart pounding, her blood rushing in her ears, her bare feet smacking the cool hard stones of the dungeon stairs. Her heart was in her throat, and her hair flew behind her. Envelopes rained down around her head, she put her hands over her head and they made tiny bloody cuts on the backs of her hands.

A huge wooden door slammed behind her. She was alone in the dark—until she saw Cat coming towards her.

"Cat," she gasped. "We're in danger! We need to get out of here!"

Cat walked closer.

"Cat, come on! We've gotta go!"

Cat smiled, sly and angry.

"Cat?"

Cat split down the middle, her skin peeling away. Jamie wanted to scream. Underneath the skin was not blood and fleshy organs but Lincha. *That's* when Jamie shrieked.

Headmistress Hilda appeared next to him. She high-fived him and pointed her wand at Jamie. "Sorry darling. Time to die." Jamie fell to the ground, the raining letters whispering their secrets in her ears while Rosie's voice called her selfish over and over again. Then she was her foster mother, screaming at her to get her suitcase, telling her she was impure. Everyone was screaming at once. The noise was deafening, and then just like that it stopped.

She looked up, to see Tab, Cat, and Jane standing back to back to back pointing their wands at the monsters. Jamie watched Lincha and Headmistress Hilda disappear, and all the letters flatten to the ground.

"Cat, Tab, Jane, thank you!" She grabbed Cat's hand, their fingers interlacing briefly. But Cat was made of a cloud. She couldn't grab on, she couldn't hold on to her sister. And she realized as Cat and Tab and Jane disappeared, not ever. Cat was destined for big things, she could do it all. She could out-talk any teacher in as many languages as exist, she could do amazing magic tricks, she could save Jamie's butt any day

120

of the week. And all Jamie was destined for was killing her own flesh and blood.

Jamie curled up and cried. The dungeon was dark and empty. Which was exactly how she felt.

* * *

When Jamie woke, she was exhausted, more tired than before she fell asleep. It was still slightly dark, and there were dark tear spots all over her pillow.

She looked over at Cat, who was fast asleep, and Rosie who was tossing and turning in her bed. Cat was going to be great, she'd be someone's hero one day. And Jamie would still be here, teaching mediocre magic students how to turn a frog into a rat.

She'd always known this, and now it was playing out for real. She was the one who needed to kill Lincha, but Cat was the one who was smart enough to release him. Cat was smart and kind and cunning, she would be famous and amazing one day, and Jamie wouldn't. It hurt, but it was right.

29

'Tis the Season to Rebel

January seemed to be the month for rebellion. For Jamie, it was bringing home a cat. For Rosie, it was ignoring Jamie completely, and for Cat, well, Jamie wasn't sure. Cat still seemed to be completely perfect, despite what had transpired in her life.

Jamie and Tab had met at one of the on-campus Cafes. It was called appropriately enough, "The Cat Café," and had cats roaming around it like flies roaming around a pile of dog poop. Well, maybe that wasn't the best image to give herself as she walked into her first date ever. For once, Jamie had dressed to impress. Her hair was combed, her jeans were unfaded blue and not ripped, and her dark purple sweater was conspicuously free of moth holes.

Tab picked up a dark-pink-and-blue cat and kissed it on the nose. "Hi Snuggles!" she said, and placed him on what Jamie assumed was their table. She picked up a dark gray and light purple kitten who looked maybe two months old. She handed her to Jamie and sat down. A man with cocoa skin, freckles and a scraggily beard soon came up and took their order.

Tab insisted that they *Must not get the hot chocolate because entire societies will collapse if we do.* Their waiter winked at Tab as he left with an order for two iced chocolate buns, one hot cider and one vanilla milkshake.

"This place is adorable," said Jamie, stroking a kitten, who was purring and cuddling on her lap. "I love it here."

Tab grinned. "Yeah, my dad runs it. You can take any cat home. Our huge fat cat has given birth three times in the three years we've had her. That one's named Kaze. You can take her home if you want."

Jamie held the cat close. She was adorable. "Y'know, I think I will."

Tab beamed. The chocolate iced buns looked warm, and filled with oozy cream and delicious thick icing.

Jamie's milkshake was tall and inviting, with a pile of whipped cream and tiny rainbow sprinkles on top. "Whoah," she said, indulging in the sweet, sweet smells. She took a bite of the giant iced bun, squirting cream out the other side. Jamie nearly melted into the seat. It was warm and gooey, with beautiful cream and smooth cake, and amazing chocolatey flavor.

"Good right?" said Tab. She was already halfway through her iced bun, and her hot cider was half drained.

Jamie snickered.

"Whaaat? I'm hungry! And a fast eater."

Jamie bumped her shoulder against Tab's, smiling. "So... what time are you from anyway?"

The two of them laughed and joked and ordered two more iced buns. When they were full, Tab waved at Jamie to follow her, grabbing Snuggles while Jamie grabbed Kaze. They went into the kitchen, which was beautiful and shiny, everyone at their stations working hard. Jamie was mesmerized. But this wasn't what Tab had in mind.

The pantry. It smelled sugary and had giant shelves of food. They came upon the giant hot chocolate machine. It was a bubbling vat of hot chocolate like in Willy Wonka's chocolate factory. "Wow," said Jamie, raking her fingers through her short hair.

"Come on!" Tab held up a mug.

"Really?" said Jamie, drumming her fingers on her tight jeans. She leaned in and whispered, "Won't we get in trouble?"

Tab shrugged, and Jamie dipped a cup in the tub. She took a sip, and spit it out.

"I told you it was terrible."

Jamie laughed, and Tab dropped her cup on the ground.

"Really I brought you here so you could get the recipe for iced buns so you could make it with Cat and Rosie."

Jamie grinned even though there was no way in heck she'd ever make a kindergarten crafts project with Rosie much less the most delicious thing she'd ever tasted.

"Sure, thanks!"

The two girls stared at each other, smiling. Jamie's kitten pawed at her arm. Tab handed Jamie the paper without moving her gaze. Jamie felt her phone buzzing in her pocket. She knew it was rude, but without moving her gaze, she pulled out her phone and pressed it to her ear. It was Cat.

Jamie held up a finger. Tab nodded and began placing the top on the vat of hot cocoa.

Cat was yelling although the words were muffled somewhat because she had a habit of holding her phone upside down. "Jamie? Where are you! You were due back an hour ago, we need to work on our Potions class project!"

"I'm coming, I'm coming! Jeez." She pressed the red off button.

Tab smiled sadly at Jamie. "Aww." She sighed and fake choked up.

"Parting is such sweet sorrow, etcetera..."

Jamie laughed out loud. "See you tomorrow?"

"Yeah." They walked up the stairs. Jamie walked away with the recipe and the kitten. Tab was quiet. The only sound was Jamie's boots clicking on the floor, and Tab's sneakers squeaking after them.

"Hey Jamie, you forgot something."

Jamie whipped around. Tab stood there empty handed (well, except for Snuggles).

Jamie looked to see what she could have forgotten, and then Tab grabbed her hand and she felt that bolt of electricity zap through her body again, just like when she tried to kiss Rosie. They walked out to the front door, smiling, holding hands. Jamie's stomach was all bubbly. "Bye..." With Kaze, the little kitty, firmly in her arms, she walked out on air.

That air would be removed once Cat saw the cat, and shrieked loud enough to scare the heavens.

30

Volleyball Practice

"How'd it go?" asked Cat, who was reading in a giant plush armchair with her scarf wrapped around her neck. Her long blue hair was in two neat braids, and she looked nice and cozy in her light lavender knitted sweater. Jamie by comparison was a sweaty mess.

"Water," croaked Jamie. Cat winced. Kaze brushed against Jamie's legs, and Cat walked over to pick her up.

"That bad?" said Cat.

"Water," Jamie repeated. Cat dropped Kaze to the ground and held out her hands. Jamie watched Cat's cupped palms fill with a pool of fresh water. Jamie took a sip, instantly feeling a little better.

"I take it," said Cat as Jamie slumped down the wall, "that volleyball practice was exhausting?"

Jamie nodded, wiping sweat from her brow.

About a week ago, she'd been walking back from Potions with a cauldron of bubbling pink liquid. It spilled in droplets on the ground, and just as she had the bright idea to put a lid on it, she crashed into June.

Jamie's potion splattered across the girls and the floor, and June's smoothie went flying up out of her hand, the cap coming off, pink-red liquid raining down. Chunks of banana splattered the top of Jamie's head.

"OmigodJamieareyouokay?" June talked so fast Jamie could barely understand her.

Jamie nodded.

"Itoldtheguydthattheplastictopsonthesecupswouldneverstayon,mygodwhat'sonme?"

Jamie opened her mouth to respond, but before she could—

"Heywherewereyouduringvolleyballpractice,wepickedteamsforscrimagesandstuff,you'recaptainwherewereyou?"

Jamie raised an eyebrow. *Oh yeah...* she thought. *I'm a team captain.* "Oh... That. I was, uh... sick?" The last few weeks had been so crazy, dates at the Cat Cafe with Tab, hanging out and making up for lost time with Cat, ignoring Rosie, being kept up at night by that letter. Everything that was not that seemed insignificant by comparison.

Her life had been so strange. She realized she'd been standing there like a complete and utter idiot for maybe thirty seconds without saying anything and June was giggling and poking Jamie's smoothie covered arm. "Umm, earth to Jamie?"

"Oh, yeah. It's the potion to cure some weird sickness. It's almost finished." Jamie looked June up and down. "Or at least it *was.*"

June smiled and pulled out her wand. "Nothing unfixable!" she said gleefully.

It made Jamie uncomfortable to see everyone just whip out their wands for everything. She wasn't good at any magic other than potions, and when she offered to help manually, everyone just stared.

She smiled weakly as the potion and smoothie went back into their respective containers. They both kind of looked like bubbly cough medicine. She picked up her cauldron.

June was still staring at her like she wanted to eat her. "Um, anything else?" asked Jamie, playing with her hair.

"Oh, no. But since you're feeling better, I'll see you at practice?"

Jamie felt very deer in the headlights in that moment, and she surprised herself with her answer. "Yeah, definitely."

June smiled and sipped her smoothie. Then she turned on her heel and walked away.

Jamie had to work on her ballet midterm, and over-analyze the letter to death again, but she had some time to kill. How long could volleyball practice take anyway?

Oh, how wrong she was.

* * *

"Three freaking hours!" screamed Jamie. She thought better of it a second later when her already dry throat sent back a shock of pain. "How ridiculous is that?"

Cat snorted back a laugh. "Sorry, but, maybe you should, quit? I mean, there is a lot going on with Lincha-"

Jamie cringed at his name.

"And, honestly, I really missed you, and more practices this long are just taking away time. With you."

Jamie sensed the "While I still can." But she dismissed it just the same. "Well, I'd love to not do more of those practices, but these girls are my friends. I don't want to let them down."

Cat blew a strand of hair up off her forehead. "Okay," she sighed. "Just bring a water-bottle next time."

Jamie smiled and picked up her bright blue duffel bag, slinging it over her shoulder and fake rolling her eyes at her twin, "Okay, M*om*."

Cat grinned back. It felt like they were drifting apart, which hurt, but she also knew it was part of growing up and having a sister.

Right?

* * *

By some miracle, the girls won the first game against the team from 1924, and the boys beat 2105. June informed Jamie and Rosie and Tab, who were all on the team, that there would be a party at dorm building two the next night, and they all just *had to come.* Jamie and Tab said they were down, but Rosie seemed distant.

June basically begged Rosie to come, so she caved, because who could refuse June? Who could refuse her piercing eyes, and kind smile? Could Cat come, too? "Of course!" June exclaimed. "Everyone's invited!"

Everyone indeed. When Jamie and Cat walked in, it was clear that June *was not kidding.* The dorm was so stuffed full Jamie nearly had an asthma attack. That is, she would have if she actually had asthma.

The host of the party seemed to be a friend-but-not-a-friend of Emily's named George. When Cat heard this, her eyes darted around, and she mumbled something about finding Anna. She disappeared into the crowds and left Jamie standing there alone, waiting for something to happen.

31

Party Fight Face

Tab found Jamie pretty easily. Jamie was the only one without a jersey on. Tab tapped her on the shoulder and smiled brightly. "Hey, you made it!"

Jamie managed a watery smile. "Yeah, so did literally *everybody else.*"

Tab knocked her shoulder against Jamie's. "Oh, a ton of people will clear out in a few minutes."

Jamie raised one eyebrow. "Why is that, exactly?"

Tab's smiled knowingly and said, "You'll see in three, two, one..." She pointed to the couch, where George stood, trying to get everyone's attention.

"People! People! Let's play that good old game. Spin the bottle!" Jamie's body clenched in fear which Tab noticed, of course. "Hey, you okay?"

"Yeah. I'll be fine." The crowd was beginning to clear out like there had been a nuclear explosion, Cat among them. Jamie grabbed her sister's arm, "Oh, no! You are *not* leaving me here to do this alone."

Cat looked like she was going to throw up.

"Cat, this is not the time to freak out."

"Jamie, this is the perfect time to freak out."

It was hard to disagree. Tab pulled the twins into the circle of people that had formed. Jamie noticed Cat noticing that Anna had escaped.

Lucky, thought Jamie glumly. Cat sighed next to her.

George had placed the empty soda bottle in the center of the weird bean-shaped circle of maybe fifteen people. Jamie sat directly across from Rosie, who had not managed to make it out and back to the safety of their dorm. Or so it seemed. The bottle spun around the circle. Jamie's heart jumped into her throat each time the inside of the bottle revealed itself to her as it spun. Cat seemed mesmerized. All the girls held their breath. The truth is Jamie could have cared less about who the stupid bottle landed on as long as it wasn't her.

It missed her by just three people, landing on a girl with bright yellow eyes and dark green hair who was the recipient of the first kiss of the evening. The kiss lasted less than half a second, but the girl still pulled away in a fit of embarrassed giggles, turning to her friend, who made little kissy noises. Jamie felt sorry for her, although it *was* kind of funny.

The bottle was spun again, and again, never landing on Jamie. But it did land on Tab, who was forced to kiss a greasy pimply boy with hair like dirty hay for a brief fraction of a second. But that was nothing compared with what happened next.

Tab, as the unlucky recipient of the bottle's whim, now got to spin. Jamie watched the bottle as it twirled around the circle. This time it landed on Rosie.

Jamie felt all the air leave her body.

Tab looked at Jamie with a look that said, "Is this okay?" Jamie swallowed, made the palest smile ever, and put a thumb up.

Tab shrugged, and leaned across the circle. Rosie pressed her lips against Tab's and stayed there. This was the longest kiss by far, maybe ten seconds. Jamie felt fury boiling up, red hot and clouding her vision, spilling over the sides of the cauldron that contained it. Rosie was doing this to simply spite her, and she was doing an excellent job. The kiss continued, boys were cheering, girls were oohing, and Cat was staring, mouth open, aghast. She looked over at Jamie, who didn't even try to hide her anger.

Tab pulled back, upset at Rosie, who smiled a smug smile in Jamie's direction.

Jamie wasn't sure if her brain even processed the thought before she did what she did next. She dove all the way across the circle, and her fist made perfect contact with Rosie's nose, and she heard screams.

Tab and Cat: "Jamie no!"

Most boys: "Fight! Fight!"

Most girls: "Augh!"

Rosie: "Jamie, what…"

Then the yelling stopped. Jamie had some of Rosie's nose bleed on her fist, and the floor seemed to not be under her anymore. The punch had relieved so much of her pain and anger that it felt like she could fly.

She opened her eyes one at a time, afraid to see the mess she'd created. Everyone was staring up at her in disbelief. But they were all standing for some reason, which was odd to say the least, since most were taller than she. Also, she was also almost certain she'd landed on her knees when she'd dived across the circle.

But looking down at them, she realized why. She was flying.

32

Flying Out On Her Own

The first thought she had when Jamie realized she could fly, was *I can get out of here and no one can catch me.* So she flew. It came naturally, like breathing. Or maybe she was just desperate to get out and her instincts acted accordingly.

People called out and yelled after her. Someone blocked the door, George, she assumed. She began to panic and started to float down to earth. Rosie ran to join him, nose crooked and gushing blood. Her glasses had fallen off, and her lavender mane was a mess. Jamie's anger had shot her right up into the sky. She held out her hands in front of her, which she noticed were glowing purple. *I need to get out.*

As she thought that, the door shattered into a million splinters, and she flew out like a bullet. Shooting into the sky, she let the anger boil inside her body. The dome that acted like a sky for The Academy was so close her fingertips were just inches from it. She wanted to use this new-found power to shatter the sky, to shatter everything.

Then she heard a voice in her head.

Lincha's voice.

Jamie, do it, break the dome, let me wreak havoc on The Academy so we can rule together. Do it, shatter what must be shattered.

Lincha's voice sparked new anger in her stomach, an anger at feeling worthless. The powers were obviously the doing of Lincha, he had planted them there, she knew that having powerful magic was too good to be true. *What have you done to me?* **Nothing, my darling daughter, this power is all you.** Jamie wanted to punch him for calling her that. *But-* **The anger inside of you has activated the demon powers I've passed down to you.** *How do I get rid of them?* **I'm not telling you.** *I don't want to hurt The Academy.* **But you do. You know you do, and you will. There's no one to stop you.** *There's me. And Cat will find me soon.* **But will she?** *Yes. And anyway, I won't let you make me do this.* **I don't have to make you do anything. You'll start to self-destruct on your own. Like human beings do.** *Shut. Up.*

But she knew he was right. She wanted to destroy the dome that protected The Academy from the horrible world. She wanted everyone to feel the pain she felt. She began to punch the dome. Her fists glowed with magic, and cracks began appearing, and Lincha's voice got louder and louder. **Yes, do it now! SHATTER THE DOME!** Then she heard something else.

"JAMIE! COME DOWN! STOP WHAT ARE YOU DOING?" Cat. Suddenly, the glow on Jamie's hands started to flicker out, and she began to fall through the air, hearing people scream, hearing Lincha's voice playing through her head like an angry headache. **No, No, No! Stop! Get back up! Cat, don't make her do this!** Cat's voice came in loud and clear. *No.*

Jamie! I'm gonna save you!

Jamie jumped in, *Thank you.* She let herself fall, and then she felt water cover her body, a giant ball of water held her, and then the sphere of tidal waves resting on the ground exploded and left Jamie lying drenched and alone on the ground. Alone except for Cat. Cat ran over and pulled her sister to her chest, and the girls sat there. Jamie was soaking wet, Cat's once neatly combed hair was windblown, and as they sat there, they both heard Lincha's voice loud in their ears.

I'm not leaving girls, I'm staying until you let us win. The twins both had the same thought at the same time. *Then you better get comfortable.*

* * *

Jamie was still dripping wet when she and her sister arrived at the dorm. Cat and Jamie both collapsed on their respective beds, an awkward silence emanating across the room.

Jamie propped herself up on her elbows, about to say something, but then rethinking it. Cat was the first to speak. "You—magic just—it's—you're um…"

"Yes."

"It was him. Wasn't it, oh…. that piece of—"

"No, Cat, I appreciate you being mad on my behalf, but it was me. The anger I had towards Rosie released the demon magic that has always been inside of me. That's why I'm so bad at magic. You inherited our mother's magic. Which I guess would be the good magic, and I got his magic, which makes me want to destroy stuff. We need to learn to contain it."

Cat raised her eyebrows and spoke slowly from across the room. "You mean control it?"

"No," said Jamie curtly, flipping onto her back. "Contain it. It's the only way to do it. So I don't *kill everyone.*"

"But—" Cat was suddenly sitting next to her on the bed, throwing tiny spheres of bright blue magic up and popping them like bubbles. Jamie took a deep breath. Cat was literally throwing magic around in front of her, and it hurt. Jamie's hands started to glow again, and she started to float.

"Stop that," she said, in a raspy voice that was definitely hers but also definitely not hers. Cat let the balls of power slip back into her palms, and Jamie sank back to the bed and began to cry.

Cat looked horrified. "Oh Jamie, I'm sorry. Don't cry."

"Why not? The world is crumbling around us. This is the perfect time to cry. I can't think of a better time." Jamie stared at sister with tears in her eyes.

"But if you contain it, it could build up, and then it could destroy things. Like in that movie Rosie showed me with the funny snowman."

Jamie scoffed bitterly, "*Frozen* is not psychological fact."

"Well, yeah, but—"

Jamie held up a hand to stop her. "I nearly destroyed the dome, I almost let him in. I put everyone in danger. I need to have something to contain that darkness. Please, Cat."

Cat sighed while Jamie pleaded with her eyes.

"I don't know… well, okay, but only if you promise to also learn to keep and control the flying."

Jamie frowned. "Okay, tomorrow I'll start concocting some containing potions, and you go to the library to research spells."

Cat sighed again, and then they both changed out of their party clothes and went to sleep. With eyes closed, just before she drifted off, Jamie thought of a quote from her favorite comic strip. *A good compromise leaves everyone mad.*

33

Flying for Dummies

"Jamie! Calm down!" shrieked Cat.

Jamie was upset, but instead of saying anything, she pointed her hands at the nightstand, which instantly exploded (and felt good)! She laughed loudly. Cat didn't find it funny at all.

As Jamie's anger began to subside, sadness and guilt took over. Her head was filled to bursting. This was the third experiment. They had tried a potion in which Jamie had basically used everything but the kitchen sink (it turned her into a rainbow frog with warts that made Cat fall down laughing) and a spell that Cat had found in a book that looked a million years old (it made small red dots appear on her face, but she did stay up). They were now trying the same spell, but Jamie had to clear her head completely, and Cat changed the wording.

"Remember not to think about polka dots!" said Cat, pointing her wand at Jamie.

Jamie tried to banish all thought from her hot angry skull. She breathed in, and the anger seemed to lessen, and she was floating down when she heard Cat yell some nonsense and there came a bright color of lights, and then a thud and a sharp pain in her head. Now she was lying on the ground, flat on her back. Cat was also down, her skinny legs peeking from her olive green dress. They seemed to have been knocked out from under her by the purring kitten a few feet away.

Jamie reached out for the furry fiend's tail and pulled the scared creature towards her head. She flipped over onto her stomach and sat up. Cat sat on her knees there, ivory skin flushed, eyes angry.

"Stupid little Foolzer," said Cat, waving a disapproving finger at the sneaky cat. Jamie snorted as Kaze rubbed up against Cat's ankles.

"I'm sorry, a stupid *what?*" asked Jamie, doubling over in laughter.

"It's an insult in my time. It means clumsy." Cat crossed her arms. "And shut up."

"Aw, come on, Cat, she just liked the pretty lights. It wasn't really working anyway. Let's go to the dining hall and get warm cookies and some milk."

Cat smiled in a way that made Jamie think she was considering it.

"Okay, but we have to try that other potion you made that's that weird galaxy color."

Jamie sighed. "Fine. Let's go before Tab steals all the black and whites."

* * *

When they got to the dining hall there was the usual crowd around the snack table, people snatching fruits, pastries, desserts and bags of chips, with Emily's crew running the table, and Emily standing off to the side. She was smirking and counting the money from the tip jar that always had been there. Even though it was free to get an after-class snack, Jamie's lips puckered in anger.

Cat grabbed her foot and pulled her back to the ground. They walked up to the table, and saw Tab there, stuffing her pocketbook with *all* the black and white cookies. Jamie grabbed one from her purse, and snatched one from the plate for Cat. Tab stood there sheepishly, cookie crumbs falling from her over-stuffed mouth.

"Hey, you're not, like mad at me for everything that happened at the party, are you?" Jamie asked.

Tab considered. She took another bite of the cookie. "I'm not mad per se, since having an overprotective girlfriend is pretty cute—"

Jamie blushed at the word "girlfriend."

"—but you do need to explain some things to me, cuz I have no idea what happened back there."

"Okay," Jamie said.

"Okay," Tab mimicked playfully, then ran to catch up with Cat.

Jamie hurried after her, chewing on a piece of oat-covered chocolate.

"Do you think you'll go on the Headmistress's field trip to New York City 1984?" Tab was saying to Cat.

Jamie couldn't help but think, *I never want to talk to, see, or associate with her ever again, so no.* But then it hit her.

"Cat. That's it! That's it! Hilda's letter, it's a code! I know what it means! Thank you, Tab, thank you, thank you so much!" Jamie grabbed Cat's wrist and said, "Let's go!" The two of them had gone no more than twenty feet when Jamie suddenly turned around and ran back to Tab, planting a small kiss on her cheek before hustling off again.

When Jamie reached her dorm, Cat was already there, underlining words on Hilda's letter with a sharpie. Jamie leaned over to see if she had been right.

2\12\84

Dearest <u>Lincha</u>,

I wish we could <u>meet in</u> person, but there are <u>new</u> chairs being installed in the teachers' Lounge. I'm being driven up the wall. I had to get some of those <u>York</u> Peppermint patties shipped in from the <u>city</u>, to calm myself.

I need to <u>look at</u> getting some new boots, I've had these since <u>the</u> last <u>date</u> I had with you.

Sincerely

Hilda

The girls looked at each other in shock. "We need to go on that trip," they said together.

34

Control at Last

J amie sat slumped at the desk, surrounded by torn, balled up pieces of paper on the floor. She was half asleep. She heard the door slam, and then Rosie came in. Jamie was so tired. Her body was like a dead caterpillar collapsed against the desk.

The girls hadn't talked for two solid weeks. It was awful. Jamie was too tired for a full on reconciliation now, but maybe they could build up to one. She had enough energy for a decent "I'm sorry, can we talk more tomorrow" conversation. Besides, she had just been reacting to *Rosie* being jerky. It wasn't up to her to apologize, was it?

"Rosie?" she said sleepily.

Rosie sighed, as if she'd been hoping to sneak by without anyone noticing.

Jamie realized that it was going to be up to her. "Rosie, wait! I hate that we're not talking. I know I shouldn't have punched you. That was wrong. But you have to understand I had a lot going on. You made me so mad. I'm not proud of it or anything, but I really don't want to fight anymore."

Rosie turned and faced her. She looked Jamie dead in her eyes, anger simmering behind the beautiful lavender of her shadowy irises.

"You know what's messed up?" Rosie said. "You can't even apologize to me. You're so proud you can't even just say you're sorry. You're the only one at fault here. I tried to tell you how I was feeling, and you made it all about you.

"And another thing, I miss you so much. I want to stay your friend so badly. But you can't even let your guard down for one second to say you're sorry. And no matter what you say, your night that night couldn't have been worse than mine."

Jamie felt herself starting to float, but for once didn't feel blind with rage or without control. In fact, she felt like she had control. She tried a pirouette in the air just to see.

It worked. Rosie was still talking. "So what, your dad ran away. I have had way worse things happen to me."

Ah. Thought Jamie, *Cat lied too.* She floated down, and then floated up. She was having fun with her control, and Rosie was still going on and on.

"You know what Rosie, I am sorry. I'm sorry that Cat lied. She should have told you what really happened that night. I won't apologize for any actions other than the punch, but I also want to mention that I'm obviously not the only self-absorbed one, because you like the sound of your own voice so much you didn't even notice I've been flying all this time.

"So thank you for being here for this moment of discovery, we'll talk more tomorrow and goodnight." Jamie flew to her bed, snuggled under the blanket, and fell asleep, counting sheep for maybe a minute—despite Rosie's ongoing harangue.

* * *

Oh Jamie, I remember the thrill of being in control for the first time. Heavenly feeling isn't it?

Jamie was standing in the forest of golden trees, the sky a blue like her hair, the grass a green like her eyes. Lincha stood against a tree suddenly. Appearing like he'd been there all along.

"It is. Now get out of my head. Get out of my dreams, and get out of my life."

Lincha smirked.

"I can't. Sorry. Oh, so sad."

Jamie scowled.

"Did your sister tell you everything?"

Jamie let her hands glow with magic, ready to strike. Lincha just chuckled. Jamie was lifted up and turned upside-down.

"You don't want to fight me Jamie. I have more experience. I'm an old hand at this. You just learned control. You *will* lose."

Jamie held out her hand anyway, pulling herself from the magical aura and shooting a beam of light out of her hands and right into Lincha's eyes. He disappeared and reappeared on the other side of the forest. Jamie closed her eyes so tight they hurt, popping up suddenly next to her father. He looked surprised at her power.

"Don't underestimate me," she said, shooting a beam into Lincha's stomach. He doubled over. They were at an impasse, they could fight in this dream forever, with Jamie's experience growing by the second. But the more she waited, the more another idea hit her.

"I just realized something."

"What?"

"I can wake up."

"Jamie!"

Jamie opened her eyes, and Cat was standing over her with a worried expression on her face. "Are you all right?"

Jamie nodded and they sat together on the floor, feet touching, staring into each other's eyes like it was the only thing they knew how to do.

Cat cocked her head to the side. "What?"

"The trip is to 1984 New York. Isn't that where our older sister lives?"

"Yes."

"You don't seem happy about it," Jamie said, and when Cat didn't respond, added, "Don't you want to meet her?"

Cat stayed quiet, tucking her knees to her chest.

"I mean, she doesn't want to be found obviously. So, maybe...no. I just can't wrap my head around the idea of her having a daughter. I don't know why, but it feels, wrong." Jamie knew that Cat wasn't accustomed to unmarried women having children and all that other stuff, so she huffed all her outrage and feminist anger out her nose. She knew even her and Tab being together probably bugged Cat although they hadn't talked about it. Not yet anyway.

"I still think we should try to find her. If she shuts us out, she shuts us out. We don't have to beg. Okay? Don't you at least want to meet our niece? She's like half named after you!"

Cat smiled a little. Jamie knocked her shoulder against her sister's.

"So, did you finish your homework? "

"Oh potato skins! I forgot!" Jamie jumped up, shuffling through the papers on the floor and on her desk. When she saw the grin on her sister's face, she put her hands on her hips. "What's so funny?"

"I say that phrase in every language I know."

35

Travel to New York City

J amie wasn't sure what to pack for a trip. What do you pack when you are reuniting with a long lost sister, destroying an evil plan orchestrated by your father and the head of school, and trying long distance to patch together your relationship with a girl you haven't talked to for weeks?

"Layers," said Cat, when asked about Jamie's predicament.

"That's helpful how?" asked Jamie from the ceiling. Her hair floated down from her head as she gestured upside down.

"Well, you don't want to worry about being cold on top of everything else," said Cat from somewhere below Jamie's left ear.

Jamie floated down and landed cross legged on her suitcase.

Cat was by the dresser, holding up a pair of pants. "What do you think?" she asked.

Jamie tilted her head to the side and blinked.

"Perfect. Lovely." Jamie actually thought they were the ugliest pants she'd ever seen, but the smile Cat gave her was powerful enough to light up a thousand bulbs.

Cat packed the pants away, then moved on to shoes.

"So, layers huh?"

Cat nodded, and Jamie dragged her suitcase to the door.

Jamie and Cat were not on the same travel schedule, but Tab and Jamie both were traveling with Ms. Havlu. Cat would be following them with Professor Delasouf, the Cooking, Sewing and Other Human Skills teacher. Tab flung herself into Jamie's arms as soon as she saw Jamie. Jamie wondered if it was possible for Tab's curls to be even shinier and curlier, or for her freckles to have multiplied by ten. She smelled like roses and ocean breeze.

Tab whispered quietly in Jamie's ear, "I missed you. I'm glad we get to hang out this week." They stopped hugging, and Jamie grabbed Tab's hand, as Ms. Havlu gathered them to start the time travel. The bus was ready to go, but the students were scattered all over the place.

Tab shrugged at Jamie as they boarded the bus. They clasped hands again when the bus was sucked up through the vortex all the way to 1984.

* * *

Jamie had been pretty comfortable with time travel during the midterm, but this time (ha ha) she felt sick to her stomach. Tab's hand was still in hers when they landed, but Jamie immediately leaned across her seat and barfed all over the aisle. Tab gasped. Some kids said "ew" or giggled. A few looked like they would throw up themselves. Most just held their noses or tried to get Ms. Havlu's attention.

Jamie was red as a beet and kind of pale at the same time. Ms. Havlu waved her wand and the mess on the floor vanished. Tab was still as stone, as was everyone across the aisle. Ms. Havlu shuffled everyone off the bus, including Tab, who shot Jamie a sympathetic look as she stepped off.

Ms. Havlu came over wrapped her arm around the poor hunched over girl, and patted her head sympathetically. While she was comforting her, another bus appeared on the other side of the original bus, and there was a loud scream.

A boy's leg had been crushed under the bus tire. The children on the other bus had their noses and faces pressed up against the window, including Cat, who saw Jamie and winked. Jamie closed her eyes so tight it hurt, and thought about herself on the other bus. She popped out of her spot on the ground and onto the other bus. She was leaning against Cat embarrassingly close, and when she recoiled, Cat grabbed her shirt so she wouldn't fall into the aisle.

"What's with the wink?" said Jamie, the taste of puke still fresh in her mouth, her shirt sagging where Cat had pulled it.

"Oh, let's just say I created a bit of chaos to give us some time. This should free us up to find," she fake coughed into her pale pink sleeve, "our sister and niece, plus follow Headmistress Hilda everywhere." A winking smile stretching across her pale cheeks. Jamie hugged her sister. She really was the best. Jamie had one more question.

"But why did you crush that kid's leg under the bus? Couldn't you have done something less, uhh, painful?"

Cat's laugh rang out. Heads up and down the aisle turned to look at the two girls, one of whom was hooting with laughter. Jamie blurted out the first thing she thought of.

"And the duck says, got any grapes?" She flushed bright pink. Everyone smirked and giggled, then turned back around to look at the kid with a crushed leg.

"He's agreed to my conditions. I'll fix up his leg with a little spell I learned."

Jamie raised her eyebrows. "And that's going to work? What's the catch?"

"Well, I've been doing some research…"

Jamie crinkled her nose, knowing there was something bad coming.

"We should have figured this out a long time ago. You are really talented at potions, you haven't found your element yet, even though I have, and all *witch* twins get the same element at the same time. So we should have been suspicious before, *especially* after we learned about Lincha."

Now the teachers were herding the students off the bus. Jamie held tight to her backpack straps as Cat grabbed her hand. "You mean, after *you* knew about Lincha."

"Well," said Cat as they passed two giggly girls singing show tunes loudly, "I had more important things on my mind than whether or not you had demon powers at the time. Anyway, I need you to whip up a little potion for him to drink. It's gonna contain a little demon magic because all of them do. I just thought if I told you, you'd stop making potions, and you love doing that! I need your help."

Jamie thought about this for a second.

She hated the way her demon powers took over her body and mind, but she did love making potions, and she loved her sister.

"Okay, but just know I wish you hadn't told me that."

Cat grinned and hugged Jamie, pulling back seconds later.

"Whoof! Your breath smells awful!" she gasped, then smiled and poked Jamie's arm.

36

Enter Charlotte and Kitty

"Y ou ready?" asked Cat as they stood outside a large brownstone that had flower boxes spilling over with long chains of lavenders and lilacs. Jamie swallowed and nodded. The doorbell was shaped like a peace sign and the windows had posters taped on them.

On the door there was a child's drawing, with "Sport uwr trups" written in sloppy crayon. The tape was coming unstuck from the door and, underneath, the paint was peeling from the wood. Jamie reached out for the doorbell, but pulled back a few seconds later, reconsidering.

"Together?" asked Cat, taking Jamie's hand.

"Sure," said Jamie, letting Cat guide her trembling hand to the bell. They pressed it, and a Beatles song started to play. "Here comes the sun, do, do, do…" Jamie smiled and sang along quietly while Cat just looked on, bemused.

Cat had insisted they dress their best for this, so Jamie had pulled on a dark purple t-shirt, her favorite sweatshirt and some dark leggings. Cat was wearing a dark pink winter sweater, an ivory skirt and long white stockings. Jamie looked her sister's clothes enviously, wishing her own clothes were nicer.

"Who is it?" asked a crackly voice over the intercom.

Cat said, "It's Jamison and Cathrine. We're here to see Charlotte and Kitty James?"

There was a static sound for a few seconds, then the voice came back, quavering this time.

"I... don't really want you to come in."

Cat looked crestfallen.

Jamie pressed the talk button again.

"Charlotte, we're sorry it took so long, and sorry to spring this on you, but we're your sisters. Let us in."

There was a long, horrible silence, and then they were buzzed in. Inside, the hall was lined with tile, smooth clean tile that reflected the shininess of Jamie's leather boots. All of a sudden there was a blur of blue plaid and braids running towards the two girls. They both shrieked in shock, and Cat even tripped over her feet and fell on her butt as the blur sat on her stomach. A millisecond later it pulled her up off the floor and brushed her skirt off with tiny hands too fast to even comprehend.

Before Jamie could get a better look at the blur, a door opened at the end of the hall and their older sister walked through.

* * *

Charlotte looked almost nothing like Jamie and Cat. Jamie noticed this first, after noticing how fast Kitty was. Charlotte had wide eyes, dark silver that faded to gold. Her skin was the same pale peach color as the twins, but it had more than just ten or so freckles covering it. She wore big brown and yellow leopard print glasses that slid down her nose. Her very long bright red hair was in a messy ponytail, her baggy tie-dye tank top and cutoff blue jeans a casual contrast to what the girls were wearing.

But she was the very essence of cool, with the hand-sewn patches on her shorts and her loosely tied hair. Even her aura radiated cool (Mrs. Havlu had been teaching them to notice people's auras so they could tell what kind of potion would help them relax or get into the groove of things). Cat regarded Charlotte warily, as if she were scared that she might pull a knife out or something. Jamie grabbed her hand and squeezed. Charlotte took a deep breath and said in a fluttery voice, "This certainly is a surprise. Please." She beckoned them to follow her.

Charlotte and Kitty the Blur led them into the what Jamie guessed was the living room. Cat sat down on a loveseat, legs crossed, back rigid, head up. Jamie sat next to her and picked up her hand, squeezing it tight.

"So," said Charlotte, tapping her fingers on her leg, looking from one sister to the other, not at all paying attention to her daughter, who was running around making the world's fastest sandwich. "You must be Jamison. And you're Cathrine."

Cat said, "Just Cat and Jamie is fine. "

Jamie said, "How did you know who was who?"

"Well, I'm psychic, for one thing, but also Jamie is kind of a hardcore name and no offense, but you kind of look the part."

Jamie flushed. She had never used that word to describe herself. It sounded too real for her.

Charlotte noticed her little sister's discomfort. "Omigosh, I'm sorry. That was rude, wasn't it? Why did I even say that?"

The last thing Jamie wanted was for her older sister to feel responsible for making this awkward. "No, it's fine. Really."

There was an awkward silence during which Jamie took a good look at Kitty, who had finally settled down a bit, her restless hand held firmly by her mother. Kitty was her niece, Jamie thought. It was crazy, she had a niece. Someone whose grandmother was her mother, whose mother was her sister. Just months ago she didn't think she would ever have even one person related to her, and yet here in this room were three people who had the same blood running through their veins she did.

Kitty was five, or so Hilda had said, and she had summer-kissed skin and hair that was in a million tiny braids that swung around when she moved (which was about every five seconds). Her eyes were such a deep shade of pink they were almost red. She had rosy cheeks and Jamie decided after giving her a full look over that she was the cutest human being she'd ever seen.

After a few moments Charlotte got up and went to the kitchen and came back with a paper plate of golden Oreos.

"Want some? I keep them hidden in the freezer."

Jamie and Cat looked at each other and laughed.

"What?"

The girls turned to their older sister with smiles. "We brought some with us," said Cat, digging into the bag they'd brought, and pulling out a package. Then they all laughed and took one.

* * *

The hotel where the students were staying was chaos. More specifically the gift shop was. Jamie pushed through the crowd of people in a frantic Valentine's Day induced panic. She'd found a cheap necklace and a cheesy card to get Tab, and she had to pay before breakfast. Or at least she had plans to.

She was almost to the cash register when she rammed right into someone.

"Hey! Watch where you're—" It was Tab. They stood, staring at each other, trying to think of excuses. Then Tab started laughing and pointing at the gifts in Jamie's hand. Jamie looked at what Tab had and started to giggle. They were both holding the same cheesy card and same cheap necklace.

They laughed, then dropped the cheap gifts and walked to breakfast. Jamie took Tab's hand, instantly getting that electric feeling again.

They sat next to each other at Cat's table and split a muffin in two.

"You two are too cute," said Cat, buttering her toast, and flipping the pages of a magazine. Jamie smiled, thinking, *This is exactly where I belong.*

The breakfast continued for what felt like years but also seconds. Afterwards, they went off briefly to their respective rooms, then met in the lobby where the group was getting together for the field trip. The art museum.

The girls talked and laughed all the way there, with Jamie pointing out different streets she remembered from living there long ago. Or she guessed she wouldn't live there for a long time.

"And that's where I learned to ice skate!" said Tab mimicking Jamie's excited tone. "And that's where I—" She couldn't finish before collapsing into giggles. Jamie wished in that moment that Tab would never stop talking like she thought Jamie was the best person in the world.

Inside the museum there were huge echoing halls, marble floors and statues of naked people that were both slightly embarrassing to look at and impossible to look away from. Jamie's shoes slid on the floors while the clambering of children bounced off the walls and Tab's squawky laughter echoed through the halls.

She was feeling both cheesy and mushy. Maybe it was because it was Valentine's Day and she had the best sort of girlfriend in the world, or maybe it was because she, Charlotte and Cat all loved frozen golden Oreos and Queen (the band was ahead of Charlotte's time but in a way that made it even more special). Kitty dragged Jamie to her bedroom at one point while Charlotte and Cat were chatting away in Spanish, and they played with her Barbies (she had dyed their hair in various colors). There was one that she'd created that looked weirdly like Jamie. When Jamie asked about it, Kitty just shrugged.

"I just wanted to make her. Don't know why. I think I made her for you." Kitty handed her the doll, and went back to brushing out the Rockstar Barbie's hair. Jamie tucked it into her tote bag and still had it in there.

Back at the museum, she got bored and grabbed Tab's hand, then pulled her along until they arrived in a tiny room. Jamie looked around and they saw a janitor walking towards them.

Jamie had seen this janitor before, but she'd been too giggly and happy to really to look at him. Now she looked harder and felt a pit of despair replace the bubbly electricity she'd been feeling only seconds ago.

"Tab, run. *Run!*" Tab let go of her hand and ran. Lincha held up a hand and Jamie stiffened and fell to the floor. She heard this weird sound like heels clicking across tile. The last thing she saw before her eyes drooped was Headmistress Hilda's devilish grin and Lincha's hands light up. Then the room exploded and everything went black.

V

Spring

Jamie and Cat

37

Cat

The girl in the white casket wasn't Jamie. First of all Jamie would *never ever* wear that dress. Cat even smirked a little as she stood over her "sister's" corpse. She knew it wasn't real from the second Hilda walked out of the broken down building with a fake sad expression on her face (what a phony that stupid Hilda was). But she now had proof.

Not only could Cat practically *smell* the demon magic on the fallen building, Headmistress Hilda was a horrible actress *and* the world hadn't exploded (which is what Cat assumed would happen if Jamie had *actually* died).

Tab was so distraught that getting answers out of her was impossible, and Rosie stayed in bed for weeks, crying and saying over and over, "I wish I hadn't fought with her." Cat though was still the same which made the other children wonder and whisper:

"Did she kill her own sister?"

"I heard she blew up the building herself."

"She's in shock."

"Is she a demon?"

"Is she heartless?"

"Were they even really sisters?"

All of these accusations were completely stupid, of course, but they got even louder while Cat stood over "Jamie's" casket not crying. If she yelled something like "IMPOSTER!" very loudly in the middle of the chapel then people would think she was insane and they'd drag her screaming out of the school in a straightjacket. If they didn't do it of their own accord, Headmistress Hilda would make them. Then she'd go where Jamie had gone. Although she really wanted to.

Cat had always thought that her super power (other than her actual powers) was noticing things. And since Jamie was her identical twin, she'd noticed every single thing that was a difference between the two girls. In those observations lay her proof.

First of all, the freckles. Before the falling out, Rosie's nicknames for the twins had been "Lucky" (Cat) and "Unlucky" (Jamie) because of the innocent comment Cat had made one day about the number of freckles they both had. Jamie had unlucky thirteen and Cat had fourteen, which was a multiple of the lucky number seven. The Jamie in the casket had just twelve freckles. Second, the hair. Jamie's hair was navy with five streaks of ocean blue. The Jamie in the casket had ocean blue hair and seven streaks of navy.

So Jamie wasn't dead. At least not in this form. Cat moved away from the casket and sat next to Charlotte, who was desperately trying to keep her tears in. Cat wanted to hug her older sister and tell her about everything.

But she couldn't.

Not because she didn't want to. She did. Desperately. It just wasn't fair to get Charlotte all involved in… whatever this was. Maybe that was dumb and too noble for her own good, but she felt very strongly about it.

Kitty was there. She didn't look sad either, likely because she didn't understand what was happening. Still, it made Cat happy, as if she'd found someone who understood *her*.

The worst part was she had to give a eulogy. It was awful—truly dreadful. Everyone looking at her, everyone judging her, no one understanding why on earth this person, the person who had been this dead girl's *twin sister*, once part of the same egg as this dead girl, wasn't even *crying*.

But she delivered it anyway. And toward the end, with all eyes on her, she did in fact manage to produce a big fat tear that rolled dramatically down her cheek. It was because Headmistress Hilda was looking at her in a way that made her think that while her sister wasn't dead, she might not ever see her again.

38

Jamie

If they didn't kill Jamie first, the smell in here would.

It was a mixture of urine, the mold that crept in the cracks of the walls, and the angry sweat that poured down her head at night when the nightmares snuck into her head. Most of her bad dreams included Cat, some of them didn't. A lot of them included Tab, who she would be sitting next to, but when she tried to hold her hand would morph into Hilda. When she woke up, Cat would be standing on a cliff, and Jamie would be below her, watching.

"Cat! I'm down here!" she would yell over and over again. But Cat would just stare out at the sea until Jamie woke up.

Because of the nightmares, she tried not to think too much before she went to sleep, to not imagine what Cat was doing, what Tab was doing, what her father and headmistress were planning to do to her. She felt like a cliché, using a stone to carve tally marks onto the walls.

She cried, a lot, letting loose her emotions when they couldn't hear her. She desperately tried to contact Cat in her mind, tried to contact anyone, even *Lincha* who might tell her what was going on.

Jamie was going crazy. No one to talk to, nothing to do. She'd only been taken with her travel bag, which contained her sketchpad, the doll Kitty had given her and her phone, which didn't work. She'd tell herself stories during the day, talking loudly, hoping someone would tell her to shut up, tell her something, make her feel like she wasn't the last person on earth. Sometimes, she sang at the top of her lungs before she went to sleep—even though she sounded like a walrus getting punched in the guts. In fact, the only evidence that there were other people in the world came from the loaves of bread and jugs of water that someone had delivered in the middle of the night and were there when she opened her eyes in the morning. Still, she craved more.

Distracting herself with stupid stuff was the only thing keeping her sane.

* * *

One morning, Jamie woke up and saw a little white mouse. She screamed and jumped, nearly falling on the floor. She picked up a stone and threw it at the tiny creature. The rock bounced off the wall and ricocheted back, hitting her between the eyes. She fell backward onto her bed. Stupid walls! She lay there until the little mouse climbed up onto her bed and poked its nose at her arm. She screamed again and floated up out of her bed. She pointed a glowing finger at it, and a beam of power hit the spot next to it. She floated down.

Tired and feeling worthless, she tried to fall back asleep.

The mouse had other ideas.

It crawled up onto her stomach, and when she woke up again it was staring into her eyes. She sighed and tried to flick it away, telling herself, "It's more afraid of you than you are of it." That didn't seem to help.

"Why can't you leave me alone!" yelled Jamie.

To her utter surprise, the mouse responded. "Why can't *you* just break through the walls with the power beam you just tried to kill me with?"

Jamie screamed. "Omigod! Am I going crazy? Did they drug my food or am I just sleep deprived or—"

The mouse rolled its eyes.

"You didn't answer my question," the mouse said, raking its little paw through the fur on its little head.

"Well, I've tried about ten times now, but it doesn't work on whatever wall I try. I think they've enchanted them. Who the heck are you anyway?"

The little mouse held out a little paw, which Jamie used two fingers to awkwardly shake.

"Theadore. And you are?"

Jamie lowered her head to the level of Theadore, saying, "I'm Jamie, and it's nice to meet you, Theadore, even if you're not real."

"Oh I'm real, real as the nose on your face." Theadore reached over and tapped Jamie's nose, which made her die a little inside. "I'm not saying you aren't crazy. But I am real."

"Well, that's very helpful," said Jamie, turning over on her stomach. Face down, she let loose a muffled scream into her pillow.

39

Cat

Somehow life went on. Despite Jamie not being there, and Rosie having lost her mind, life went on. When Cat, wanting support, tried sharing her theory of what had happened with Tab, Tab stopped her and said, "I don't want it to be true either, but... acceptance is a long process. Give it time, and it will make more sense." This was terrible advice and not the response Cat was hoping for, and she made sure to tell Tab exactly that. Tab stormed away in an angry huff.

It seemed Cat was alone in this.

She didn't like being alone.

She went to class, she talked, occasionally laughed with Anna and June while they recounted the fails of Jamie's short-lived volleyball career, but her mind was always on the puzzle. The pieces were all there but one.

Where was Jamie?

* * *

Headmistress Hilda called Cat to her office one day.

All month Cat had been getting looks from the Headmistress, not "watch your back" evil looks, but sort of "you better keep your mouth shut" looks.

When Cat showed up, the door clicked closed behind her, and at the same time her wand flew off her wrist and her phone floated out of her pocket. She tried to grab at them, but it all happened too quickly.

Headmistress Hilda stuffed the devices into her huge coat pockets, and was about to say something, when Cat laid into her.

"Why, you wrinkled hag of a woman! Don't think I don't know what you've done and who you are! You evil old witch!" Cat's voice was shrill and high, her face bright red, her hand pointing accusingly.

Hilda gestured at the chair in front of her. "Sit, Cat. Eat a brownie."

"I'm not touching your filthy brownies, in fact you can take them and—"

"Sit down, Cat!" commanded Headmistress Hilda. So Cat sat. The headmistress smoothed out the creases in her dress and stared straight into Cat's eyes.

"Cat, I will admit that I've made many sacrifices, mostly at yours and Jamie's expense…in the interest of bettering the world. And for that I am sorry, but you must know the truth. Only then will you understand, only then." She paused for dramatic effect. "And what I want to know is will you join us?"

Cat shot out of her chair in outrage, and shrieked back, "*Join* you? I wouldn't join you in a million years. I'd rather die."

Cat was angry. She was so angry it hurt. Hilda waved her hand and a large portal appeared. Cat stepped through.

It was amazing. A completely different world had materialized around her. She saw home. Grassy ground, wood and stone homes, clean air. *Home.*

But then she noticed the demons. Floating demons fighting with witches and warlocks. Suddenly everything began to deteriorate. Grassy ground shriveled away, wooden homes burned down and skies became cloudy with smoke and dust.

Headmistress Hilda spoke. "You see Cat, in what the ancient witches know to be your time, there was a long war between the demons and the witches. The fights burned villages, destroyed the world. But the witches didn't like that. So they decided in a council that they would do something that is absolutely forbidden. Change time." Cat's eyes filled with tears as she watched her home dissolve.

"Yes," continued Hilda solemnly, "they reversed time so that the demons would never get free enough to rule. I was opposed to the idea, and they called me a traitor, kicked me out of the council. I formed a group of witches who wanted to recreate the chaos that the demons had made. Our intent was to make a force strong enough to free the demons and restore the reign that had created the most good the magical world has ever known."

Hilda had a crazed look in her eyes as she drew in a deep breath. "Some witches didn't agree with overthrowing the system, so they were cast away in 1900. The only ones left were your mother, me, and Kilana. We created The Academy to enlighten children on how to fight and harness their abilities as weapons. Not to keep children away from demons, but to keep them away from older witches, who would ask questions about our school. About me."

"Wait," Cat said. "The collapsed gallery—how could you have known we'd be on that trip?" As she spoke, the truth suddenly dawned on her. "You set it up. You *meant* for Jamie to find the letter! For us to follow you!"

Hilda nodded, smiling slightly. "Actually I meant for *you* to find it. But yes. Though it took so long for you two to figure it out that I began to worry you wouldn't take the trip." Headmistress Hilda waved her hands then, and images appeared in front of Cat's wide eyes to illustrate her words. "As far as the council and every witch and warlock who is not you, Jamie and Kilana, I do not exist. Why do you understand that my name is Hilda and that I am not all you see, when the other children don't? Even I do not know that. But what I do know is that you and your sister were a threat to the plan just like your mother was. That's why I had to kill her. She was madly in love with your father, which was dangerous. *You* were dangerous. We tried to kill you both but when that didn't work, I decided to raise you here."

By now Cat was so completely gob smacked and horrified she could barely bear to keep listening. Still, she did.

"You and Jamie were onto us. There was a part of you missing that you were both desperate to unlock. Not to mention the fact that Jamie obviously had demon powers that overpowered even the best of my abilities. She was raised on anger, and that fed into her power. So Lincha took a step I didn't want him to take. He started sending the dreams ordering you to release him. Behind my back."

Headmistress Hilda closed her eyes to compose herself. Cat bit her lip so hard she tasted blood in her mouth.

"And now it's now. The now where you know everything."

The office re-materialized around them. Cat was sitting again, and sweat poured down her head but she felt cold.

"So Cat, now that you know the truth, will you join me?"

Cat hesitated.

"If you help me, I'll send you back to your time with a family who will love you. You can make all of this go away. Just help me. Join me."

Cat didn't want to live a life like this, surrounded by evil, but Jamie was her family, and there was nothing in the world that would ever convince her to hurt her.

She looked into Headmistress Hilda's dark eyes and said in a shaking but strong voice, "Never."

Hilda sighed and pulled a gleaming knife out of her drawer, testing the tip ominously against her palm.

Is that the knife she used to kill my mother? The one she will use to kill Jamie?

"Then we have a problem," Headmistress Hilda said, scraping the knife across the desk, making an awful noise. "You know too much." She wound up, and threw the knife.

Cat ducked as the blade smashed against the door, shattering the glass.

40

Jamie

Theadore came back the next night. His little paw scratched at Jamie's hand. She sighed loudly as he climbed up onto her stomach, twisting the ratty blanket up in his little claws, waiting for her to actually wake up, annoyed that she kept tossing and groaning, swatting him away.

"Jamie, Jamie! Wake up!"

As she continued trying to brush him off, he pulled on her finger. "Jamie you gotta wake up! I think I found a way out!"

Well, *that* got her attention.

Jamie jumped up so suddenly, Theadore was propelled into the wall. He bounced off and landed on the blanket next to her, slightly stunned. Gathering himself, climbing up her arm, he pointed forward like a commander. Following his silent command, she got up and walked right into a wall, falling backward onto her butt.

"Theadore, Jeez! That hurt! What are you doing?" She picked him up by his fur, and he emitted a little mouse shriek.

"I'm sorry! I'm sorry! There's a button on the wall, just press it, then it should open." Jamie got up again, with Theadore on her arm, and this time she carefully walked towards the wall. She picked up her travel bag with one hand, and extended the other to touch the wall, feeling around with a rough palm until she found the button and pressed it.

She waited.

"Theadore, this isn't—" And then the walls started to crumble. Jamie had a little flashback to a month ago, as the walls fell. She started to cry. She felt so weak. She never used to cry. But now she was getting freaked out by mice and crying at memories. What a weakling she had become.

Looking closer, she saw the walls weren't even crumbling, more like folding down rapidly. She drew in a breath and wiped her tears away with one hand. Unknowingly, she had just smeared ash on her pale cheeks. She mentally shook herself. *Come on Jamie, you can do this.* The dust and ash cleared. Instead of being outside as she expected, she was in a library.

It was a library Cat would go bananas over. The shelves were shiny brown wood. Three levels, connected by sliding ladders covered in ivy and flowers. There was a layer of dust over everything, especially the beautiful colored spines of the books, which all shone with gilt lettering on the spines. Jamie couldn't help but gape. There were mirrors on the walls, paintings, curtains, a fire in the fireplace, food on the table, doors to other rooms, a leather couch, a crystal chandelier. It was almost too good to be true.

Maybe it was. In fact, it *probably* was. There couldn't possibly be a room in this prison that whoever was running it didn't know about. But for now she would enjoy this while it lasted. She walked in a circle. And stepped on Theadore.

"OWWWWW!" he yowled.

Jamie kneeled down and picked up her little mouse, and looked him in his black beady eyes. "You are such a baby." Theadore frowned as she placed him on her shoulder. They started to explore the library. Some of the books were practically cemented to the shelf, but with a lot of pulling, she wiggled one out. She opened it up and coughed as a huge cloud of dust rose, which Theadore did not like, because he mimed fainting on her shoulder. She rolled her eyes.

She looked at the book really carefully, and started to read out loud. "Demon jewels were always kept in dark fire caverns... what?" She turned to Theadore. "I thought there were no demon books left in the world?"

Theadore shrugged.

She put the book down on the table and walked over to the mirror. She hadn't seen herself in weeks and didn't realized how dead she looked. Her eyes had gone hollow as if all the color had been sucked out of them, and there were giant bags underneath, which were now smeared with ash. Her cheeks were sunken and gray, cheekbones sticking out like knives.

Not only that but she'd lost so much weight she looked as skinny as when she was in first grade with her foster family on food stamps. Her foster siblings had nicknamed her "beanpole." At her next foster home in Chicago, her unfortunate new foster brother tried calling her that and got a welcome present of a punch in the kisser.

"Hey, quit staring in the mirror and let's *eat,*" Theadore said. It was then that Jamie realized that all the fruit was real. The libraries she'd seen before had fake fruit, but these fruit bowls were carrying real apples, bananas and grapes. They were rotten, though that didn't stop Theadore from digging in.

"Oh Theadore, gross."

The little mouse looked up from his moldy grapes and smiled

sheepishly.

"Maybe there's a spell…" she started picking books off the shelf, flipping carefully for a de-ripening spell. But nothing. She started to climb up the sleek wooden ladder and arrived on the second floor. Theadore had scurried up after her, and he climbed up her arm to her shoulder. She ran the tips of her thin fingers over the books, and walked around the platform. That's when she saw the huge wooden stand.

There was a large green-and-gold-leaf book encrusted with shimmery jewels sitting on it an angle. It said *Spells* on the cover in swirling gold script. The binding was worn and frayed.

Jamie opened the book and started flipping through the dusty, yellowed pages. The musty smell was overpowering, but she held in her breath and tried to focus on the different pictures. She flipped to a page that had a picture of a dead pig on it. She started to read the spell out loud.

"Sic redit ad priscum decus, tamen suus 'cave modo manifestat sui ipsius."

It was some kind of Latin, but while Jamie was trying to remember her *Dissecting the origins of spells* class, the book started to shake in her hand and she dropped it. Instead of falling to the floor, though, it started to float.

She stood back and watched it shake and glow. Theadore hid in the loose fabric on her shoulder. Suddenly there was a huge bang and light flew out in every direction. That was followed by the thump of the book falling to the floor.

She reached down to pick it up, and Theadore shrieked, "Don't *touch* it!"

"What a chicken."

"I'm telling you, don't touch it!"

"Why not?"

"Because I'd hate for you to be zapped to pieces. And that thing looks… weird."

As sweet as that sentiment was, she was too curious. Before she leaned any closer, she took Kitty's doll out of her bag and squeezed it. Then she picked up the book. The book had restored itself to what it must have looked like when new. The jewels were shiny and clean, the gold leaf had stopped flaking, the rips in the pages had sewn themselves back into the pages, and the yellow had gone away. Jamie let out a deep breath. "See Theadore, nothing to worry about. Now let's restore some frui-" There was a loud sound, like a door slamming open, followed by a voice. Lincha's voice. No, it couldn't be.

"Hello? Hilda, are you in here?"

Jamie froze. Theadore was scratching her shoulder and whispering, "Jamie, take the book and run!"

"Well duh, but how?" She crouched down as she heard the footsteps get closer.

"The window!" he whisper-shouted.

"Oh, I see. It's dangerous to touch the book but not to jump through the window?"

"Shut up and just do it!"

So Jamie crawled across the hardwood floors and got over to the window. Just as she reached for the latch, the ladder creaked, and Lincha appeared at the top of it. Jamie's eyes went as wide as dinner plates.

Lincha grinned devilishly.

She knew she only had a matter of seconds, so Jamie stood up and threw her full weight against the window.

41

Cat

I t was official. The world had gone crazy.

For Cat, everything was turned upside down. Jamie wasn't there. She didn't feel safe in the only place she'd ever belonged. And Rosie wasn't talking.

She moved like a zombie through her classes, hood pulled up over her hair, earbuds in her ears, playing music during her classes, walking the halls and during her restless sleep. She was almost sure that her ears had molded to fit her ear pieces. She didn't talk to anyone. Not anymore. Although people waved it off as grief, she had heard June complaining about how she never talked to her anymore. She hid in corners and shadows, curled up in her blankets at night, unable to sleep, scared of Hilda, scared of everything. She missed Jamie so much, it hurt.

She felt ridiculous, she'd spent thirteen years not seeing Jamie, so why should she miss her? But things couldn't go back to the way they were. The hurt of missing her rubbed Cat raw all over. Her body felt like it was made of pain, sometimes like it wasn't even hers.

But there were some small things that made her life the way it had been. Charlotte and Kitty were part of that small percentage of her life where she didn't feel her hurt for Jamie.

When she heard they were coming over to visit her plan was to put on a brave face for them. After all, they had lost someone too, even though they hadn't known her long.

But when her older sister and niece showed up at the dorm, and they gave her sad smiles, a brave face wasn't actually necessary. Instead, she felt a smile stretching across her face and a little of the sadness melting away. She ran to hug them. Charlotte wasn't normally a great hugger, but this hug was perfect. She was warm and smelled like the sparkle in the city sidewalks.

"Hey," said Charlotte, a smile lifting her apple rosy cheeks. Kaze brushed up against her legs, and Kitty picked her up. "¿Estás bien pequeño?*"

"Yeah, I'm fine." Cat *wasn't* fine, but she had some kind of moment of truth, because as long as she had Charlotte and Kitty and some friends, she was okay.

"You sure, absolutely sure? You know I can tell if you're not."

"Then why ask?"

"Because being physic doesn't make me invasive and immoral." She hugged her little sister again, and walked over to the little snack fridge. Kitty raced to beat her, but Charlotte snatched her daughter's scruff. Cat laughed. It was the first time she'd laughed in months.

As much as she hated people taking things from her fridge, she would never, ever complain about anything her sister did again. Charlotte pulled out some fruit and chips, then coaxed Kitty toward the couch and sat her down. It took two hands to keep her little girl down this time. She handed Kitty an apple and took a bite out of her peach.

Cat moved to the couch, and took a plum from her sister's skirt basket but didn't eat it. Just let it roll around in her palm, hoping it wouldn't drip juice onto her hand. Her whole hand tensed with the effort of not squishing it, not letting it drop. It felt like her life in a nutshell. A delicate balance. Except now her "plum" had been knocked out of her hand, and squished by Hilda's sharp heels.

"Hey, you okay?" said Charlotte.

Cat realized that she hadn't said a thing for three solid minutes. She sat with them and listened while they all made slightly depressing small talk before Kitty jumped up in excitement. She ran towards the door and reached into her little pink backpack to pull out some Barbie dolls from a Ziploc bag. Aside from the dolls, the bag contained a brush, a few tiny tubes of colored dyes, a surgical mask and five other Barbies with tiny doll curlers in their hair.

Kitty took all the stuff to the floor and started pulling out the tiny curlers. Charlotte sighed and rubbed the space between her eyes. "She's been doing this more and more, and I don't want it to become an obsession…" She paused, turning to carefully study her little girl. "Not that being a hairdresser would be the worst thing for her."

Cat nodded. Then Charlotte got quiet. She held the fuzzy peach carefully, rolling it back and forth between her hands. It was very sticky. The fact that she wasn't bothered by it bugged Cat on several levels.

"Jamie was so smart that day. She talked to Kitty like she was her best friend. She was the best. I should have asked her to babysit while I could." Charlotte looked sad.

This infuriated Cat.

She felt a warm scream fill her mouth. She choked it back. The lid on her feelings was going to blow. She had held back this scream for a while, listening to everyone use the past tense, when Jamie was completely and obviously present tense. But instead, she bit it back.

Big mistake.

"Oh, is that your roommate?"

Cat swiveled around, and there was Rosie.

Rosie was a mess. She hadn't been out of bed in weeks except to eat and use the bathroom. Her hair was knotted and awful, her bright eyes were dull and red above her gray cheeks. And now she was up. Why?

"Hi, I'm Rosie."

Cat was very confused. But she kept her temper even.

"Rosie, nice to see you up and out of bed," Cat said, her voice carrying an edge.

"I wanted to say hi to your guests."

That. Was. It. Cat had reached a boiling point. This rocket was going to blow.

"Really? You wouldn't get out of bed for a month after I begged you and cried by your bedside. And now, these people you've never met have convinced you to drag your butt up to say 'Hi'? Well you can stay in bed for all I care. I never want to speak with you again!" Cat wasn't even boiling, she was past that. She was an inferno, burning everything around her.

"And you." She turned to a terrified Charlotte. "Jamie! Isn't! Dead!" The words were so big and so loud, they filled up the entire room, pinned Charlotte to the floor and destroyed the smile on Kitty's pure little face. "She's not dead, and if you still think she is, you can all get out too! I don't want to see any of you ever again. Ever!" Then Cat's flame burned out, and she crumpled to the floor. The plum escaped her hand and rolled across the floor, coming to a stop against the glass window.

42

Jamie

Blood ran from the corner of Jamie's mouth. Her whole body hurt. Her bones felt broken. There was no light except the strained moonlight pooling on the forest floor. But that was under her, very far under her, as she was suspended in the air, with tiny shards of glass around her. She turned around in the air and faced the broken window.

She was falling, and fast, catching just a glimpse of Lincha's face above her.

As much as it hurt to be falling through the air after having literally jumped through a glass window, she found herself oddly satisfied by the split-second look she caught of her father's face. He had an expression of anger mixed with confusion and sadness—the feeling where your rug of happiness has just been pulled right out from under you. But maybe also…just a little bit of pride?

A grin worked it's way to her face. But then she realized she was still falling and decided to scream instead. So she did.

"Ahhhhhh!" Jamie felt the cold wind push against her back like a solid object. But then she remembered.

Oh yeah, I can fly.

The problem was that it was dark, and flying straight into the forest floor sounded like a concussion and a half, so she decided on the trees as her best bet. She reached out as wide as she could, until a tree branch actually scratched her palm. She closed her hand around the branch so quickly that she thought the thing would snap right off. But instead she hung there, about a hundred feet above the forest floor.

Thank god for my malnourishment, thought Jamie, as she hung like a leaf from the branch. She inched her way toward the trunk and used her feet to hook onto the rough bark. Fortunately, her feet were like alligator skin, so using them as grappling hooks was easier than it sounded. She climbed slowly down the trunk and jumped when she was ten feet off the ground. It hurt her ankles and she toppled over backwards and lay there. Not moving at seemed like her best bet at that point, so that's what she did.

"Lincha!" she heard someone yell. "What is going on here? Why are you just staring out the window like a crazy man?" It was Headmistress Hilda.

Jamie almost laughed. The irony of her teacher yelling at her father was so rich she couldn't help it. But one giggle could cost her everything. So she swallowed it.

"WHAT DO YOU MEAN JAMIE'S ESCAPED!" she heard Hilda yell, the sound of her name snapping her back to reality. "WHY ARE YOU STILL STANDING HERE? YOU *CAN* FLY YOU KNOW! GET OUT THERE!" Hilda sounded really mad.

Geez. Take a chill pill. And then, as guilt washed over her, she thought, *I can't keep treating her like a teacher. Not even in my head. She wants to kill me!*

Lincha responded meekly, "She can fly too, ya know. She's probably hundreds of miles away by now…"

"Then why are you not trying to catch up with her you little—" Hilda called him a word definitely not school appropriate.

"I-"

"GO!"

So Lincha jumped off the window ledge and started flying out into the forest rather than looking right under him. Jamie breathed a very loud sigh of relief. Maybe too loud.

"Jamie." She froze.

"I know you're down there somewhere," Hilda said, holding up her wand and lifting it like a conductor. She brought it down in one sharp movement, and before Jamie even knew what was happening, the earth beneath her trembled, and then started to break apart. Jamie felt panic well up in her and moved ever so slightly to avoid a crack that appeared near her. If she made any big moves, Hilda would see her, but if she didn't move, the forest floor would swallow her up. Double-edged sword. It was pitch black out, but Hilda's movements were visible to Jamie, so hers would probably be visible to Hilda.

She inched toward the tree, praying so hard that she thought her eyes would pop out of her skull. She held onto the tree and hoped it wouldn't fall through the ground. Then she saw some bushes.

It was a risky choice but she jumped into the bush, coming out on the other side. Surprised that it had worked, she stood up and started to run. The only reason she looked back was when she realized that her bag containing Kitty's doll had fallen from her hand in the rush.

* * *

Jamie found a pile of leaves to sleep in, and fell into a restless sleep that brought very strange dreams.

She and Cat were standing on stage, the lights bright and glaring. One of their favorite songs was playing and Cat was singing along, but her voice wasn't scratchy and choky like it usually was (they had both inherited terrible singing voices), it was smooth and beautiful. She was crying, tears dripping down her cheeks, her voice filling the air. In the audience, two people, Tab and Rosie. Tab had a wide smile on her face, happy to see Jamie, and Rosie had a scowl, angry at the world. Jamie was about to say something when the stage opened up like the forest floor and she fell through.

"Jamie! Wake up!" she yelled. Everything went black for a moment. And then she was in the forest again. And Lincha was there. Again.

"Hello Jamie," he said shakily.

That was when she realized she was awake.

43

Cat

"Miss Novice. Please pay attention to the class!"

Cat tapped her pencil on the desk, the eraser becoming a pink blur the faster she flicked the tip between her fingers.

"Miss Novice!"

Cat snapped to attention. She was very used to Jamie being called out for not paying attention—since they had the same last name, it wasn't weird to hear the teacher yelling it. Except, since Jamie didn't take this class, *she* was the one being yelled at.

"Sorry Professor," Cat said, looking somewhere over his right shoulder.

He sighed and turned back to the board, as if searching for an equation to answer his problem. "Can you please solve the example I just wrote on the board?"

Cat squinted at it. It was written like a foreign language.

But she was good at those.

She stared right at the board, drilling a hole into it with her eyes.

$+ \wedge - 8/4 = ?$

"No way she was paying attention," Emily whispered from behind her. That infuriated Cat. She huffed air out of her nose.

"Professor, the answer is zero." He nodded and turned back to the board. Cat looked back at Emily. "Don't sell her a dog, Emily. You're just a church bell in gas pipes. You think you're just the jammiest bit of jam don't you, well guess what? You're nothing but a weak little girl with a mean sauce box." Cat felt proud of pulling out all her Victorian phrases to insult Emily without getting in any trouble. She turned to Emily's grinning friend.

"You've got quite the gigglemug, well, you're just a meater, with a parish pick axe." The girl's mouth dropped.

"Fine. I was gonna be quiet, but I'm going to tell her what you just said to her," said the girl. *No*, Cat thought. *If I get in trouble, then I'll have to go to the headmistress' office. And then Hilda will see me, and, and*—it was too late.

"She told you that you were lying to me, that you were a gossip wearing extremely tight pants. She said that you thought you were an absolutely perfect young lady, but you're actually just a weak little girl with a mean mouth."

Emily was red. Cat was flushed as well. So she was surprised when Emily took a deep breath and produced a small smile.

"Look, cotton candy hair,"

"Cat."

"Whatever. You have guts and I like that. And you're clever. But I also hated your sister, dead or not, and you can't insult me like that, so let me tell you something."

"Something else?" said Cat, which made her mentally slap herself.

Why can't you just shut up for once!

"Yes."

Emily tossed her blond curls, and stared straight at Cat with her sapphire blue eyes. "No one gets away with being mean to my friends. Professor!"

A few things ran through Cat's head then. First and foremost was the heart bursting fear of getting sent to the office. It made the minutes drag on like hours. Second was the fact that Emily was getting her in trouble not because of Cat's insults toward her but because of her insults toward her friend. Who knew? Mean girl had a heart.

Nonetheless fear was overriding all other systems in Cat's brain. It seeped into her skin and curdled her blood. She sat in front of the office with tears running down her cheeks. So many tears had poured from her eyes lately that they had slowed to drips.

Her voice used to ring out when she screamed, but now it dribbled through the air. Sadness was all-encompassing. The door swung open and her heart jumped into her throat. She calmed a bit when she saw it was only George.

His green hair glowed weirdly in the fluorescent lighting, his navy irises almost bled into his pupils as they always did. Her stomach did a super flip, like a million pent-up butterflies getting let loose.

"Hey George, what's up?" she said. Her mouth moved without her permission, words spilling out one at a time and dropping to the floor. George smiled back, his white teeth bright and sharp.

"Hey Cat. What are you in for?"

"Oh, I insulted Emily, and she sent me here." Cat drummed her fingers on her thigh.

"She can do that?" He said it jokingly and almost curiously, like he was really wondering.

"Apparently," she responded bitterly. Noticing the look on his face, she quickly changed gears. "What about you?"

"Oh, got into a fight, my worthy opponent is in there, so you've got some more waiting for your punishment." He winked and walked away. Cat felt a smile light up her face.

* * *

"Do what you wish to me, Hilda. I have nothing left in this miserable life except one sister who barely exists and one who won't talk to me anymore," announced Cat as she walked in on a brave high from the encounter with George. Hilda smiled devilishly.

"Oh, I'm not doing anything to you, darling, but I do have a favor to ask."

Cat's lifted her left eyebrow in a perfect arc while narrowing her right eye. "What kind of favor?"

"Well," said the Headmistress, pulling her knife out of her drawer and scraping it on the wood desk, "it seems your clever sister escaped our slippery fingers. And by *our* I mean your pathetic father's." Hilda spit out the words as if they hurt. "But if you were to find her for us..."

Cat's immediate thought was, *Jamie escaped? Jamie escaped!*

"No way."

"Fine. I thought you might need a bit of persuasion, so here's a little incentive." Hilda pulled out a small bag and emptied its contents into Cat's palm. Cat dropped it the second it touched her, but the damage was done. She felt her fingers numbing, saw the tips of her fingernails turning coal black.

"You have twenty-two days to find her or your body will turn to carbon," Hilda said. "And," she added, seeing the look of determination on Cat's face. "So will your niece. But once you touch Jamie she will be trackable and you and your niece will heal.... Sound like a deal?"

Cat's mouth dropped open. She backed up and reached for the doorknob, then turned and ran from the office, Hilda's dark words penetrating the walls around her brain. She ran and ran and ran. When she reached her destination, she looked around. Was there anywhere else to go?

No. She looked down at her blackening fingers, and clenched them into a fist. She knocked on the door and it opened. The face behind the door was stone.

"Can you help me? Please?" whispered Cat. Her tears fell like rain. And the only thing Rosie could do was hold her while her best friend sobbed in her arms.

44

Jamie

No, no, no, no, no. I've come so far, there's no way I can lose now. No. Jamie backed away on her knees, standing quickly and backing up, ready to dash. But Lincha's face stopped her. It was calm, but a little sad, even a bit pained.

"What's wrong with you?" asked Jamie before she could stop herself.

"Nothing," he replied, shifting, moving his hands from his pockets to cross his chest. "I'm giving you a… head start."

Everything was just falling apart in every way possible. "What?" Jamie was thoroughly confused and about to cry.

Lincha stomped the ground. "Dammit Jamie, just go! I am letting you go!" He looked like he was about to cry too—almost as if he had a heart.

"But why?" Jamie asked, moving forward a few inches, crushing the leaves beneath her feet.

"I just can't do this anymore."

"Look Lincha, I don't have time to play games with you, so just tell me what's going on and then let me go."

Lincha *was* crying now, long streaks of tears running down his pale

186

cheeks. "I—"

"What?"

"I loved your mother!" he shouted, looking at the ground. "I loved her and I never wanted Hilda to kill her. And I love you and Cat and feel so bad for hurting you. Worse than you can imagine. But as you very well know it's you or me, only one of us can live, that's the demon's cross to bear.… And Hilda promised me the life I wanted. She promised me freedom. So I kept going, hurting you and hating myself for it."

Jamie was crying now, for her sister, for her mother, and secretly, for Lincha.

"I know what you must think of me, that I'm the bad guy, the most powerful, evil demon in this world. But I'm not. I'm just another self-centered angry demon in a sea of them, who is now trying to make up for lost time by giving you a chance to run! So go Jamie, run." He was really sobbing now. "Run because I love you."

Jamie was shell-shocked and confused. Angry. But also sad. Yes, sad. Sad for her dead mother, sad for her sister, sad for herself. Sad even for her living grieving father.

"Okay Dad," Jamie whispered, "I'll run."

So she did.

She ran like the wind, ran like a deer, ran so fast and hard it hurt, crashing through brush and thorns and leaves that whipped at her face and tore at her skin until she fell straight off a cliff into the pooling water under a waterfall.

* * *

After she'd landed and dried off, she built a fire. The fire wasn't big, but it was enough to warm her. Near midnight, Jamie was lying on her back near the fire, thinking about everything that had happened that day, when she heard the bushes rustle nearby.

She picked up the stick she'd been sharpening and pointed it at the woods.

Leaves began to tremble down from the tall trees. Jamie moved a little closer, yelling loudly at the trees. "Who's there?"

She saw a booted foot sticking out from one of the bushes. That was all Jamie needed. She dove into the brush, tackling the person, knocking them over, stabbing at them with her stick.

Shrieks and yells and in the midst of it Jamie caught a glimpse of her antagonist. He had a shock of white blond hair and was very pale with huge blue eyes and a thin but strong body. He was yelling, "Stop it! Stop it! Get off of me!"

Jamie stopped stabbing at him. "Why? You could be a murderer! You could be—"

"But I'm not! So get off me!"

Jamie moved her hand from his arm to his neck, finding the pressure point she had learned about in gym. It shocked him into a scream.

"Ow ow ow ow ow!" he shrieked. His voice was high, squeaky like a little boy's. Did he go to her school? She sort of recognized him but not really. Maybe Cat knew him?

"Tell me who you are!" she yelled. "Now!"

"Fine, let me up first!"

"Nuh uh, tell me first."

"I can't believe you don't recognize me!"

"Why would I?" Jamie lifted her hand from his neck.

"Because it's me!"

"Me who?" She moved her leg off his knee.

"Me, Theadore!"

45

Cat

"So let me get this straight," said Rosie while licking ice cream off the back of the spoon she was holding. "Our headmistress is evil and named Hilda. She kidnapped Jamie with the help of your *demon* father. Then put on a show that she was dead. But Jamie escaped their crazy prison probably due to *her* demon powers. And now if we don't find her in twenty-two days you *and* your five-year-old niece will turn to carbon and disintegrate?"

Cat nodded and scooped another spoonful of ice cream from the Boris and Igor's carton. "That pretty much sums it up." She took a bite and pursed her lips together. "This is my fifth bite without cookie dough! I only eat this brand for the cookie dough."

Rosie smiled sheepishly. "Um, I picked it out and ate it all."

Cat would usually have gotten a little mad hearing this, but instead just felt nostalgic for when she and Rosie could just talk without worrying about magic or anything other than the fact that the ice cream was just plain vanilla.

"Meanie."

"Yeah well… where are we gonna find her?"

It was almost midnight, and they were lying in the moonbeams with two spoons and a tub of ice cream.

"I don't know." Cat sucked on her spoon thoughtfully. "But I do know we have to go now." The tips of her fingers were already coal black. It was clear there was no time to waste.

"Okay, let's go."

Cat crammed all the clothes she could into a backpack, plus one rare magical disease book, an outdoor cookbook and a compass. Rosie packed clothes, plus a plant book, along with two canteens. Before zipping shut her backpack, Cat noticed the pale pink ribbon Rosie had given her sitting on the bedside table along with the army hat Jamie had gotten her for Christmas. It all felt like years ago.

One had come from her oldest friend, for a long time the only possession that really was *hers*. But the other was given to her by someone she loved. And what was more important? She put the hat on and wrapped the ribbon around her wrist. Before leaving, she prepared a few bowls of food for Kaze, then shut the heavy door behind her. *No looking back now.*

"I'm ready." Cat stood again in Headmistress Hilda's office, staring at the evil in her eyes. Hilda grinned her shark grin.

"Excellent. Here's a taker, it will take you to the forest where she was last seen, and you'll make your way from there." She threw a pocket watch to Cat, who caught it with a single blackened hand.

Rosie was waiting outside. They gave each other worried looks. Then they clasped hands around the watch, pressing the little button. There was a flash of light and they disappeared with the watch.

When they reappeared, everything was different than Cat would have thought. She had pictured browning leaves and dirt paths, smoky bushes and bare branches, maybe dried up rivers. A wasteland of an old forest. But there were full trees, leaves of green and flowers springing up everywhere. Long rivers that ended in shimmering starlit waterfalls. Cat thought: *Where else would Jamie be able to hide?*

And so they began to walk, the vines tangling around their ankles, leaves crunching like bones underfoot.

* * *

After two days of trekking and stopping and walking and sleeping, the black was creeping up her wrist. Rosie looked pale. Her glasses were broken in two places. Cat was hungry, cold and tired.

Night descended on the forest. They looked for a place to set up camp. Rosie complained about her empty stomach, her aching head. They were exhausted by the time they reached a clearing. Cat stopped short. Rosie bumped into her.

"Ow, why'd you stop…" Then Rosie saw him too.

Cat kind of knew him. She was sure that he'd been in at least one of her classes. But she couldn't remember seeing him in months. And what the heck was another student in The Academy doing here anyway? Where in God's name were they?

He had bright blond hair that stood up on his head and arms like fur. His eyes were a piercing blue and his skin was pale like off-white paint. He was nursing a deep gash in his shoulder. Normally the blood would have scared her, but she was so thrown by seeing someone she sort of knew in these desolate woods after days of walking that she barely noticed.

"Where did you—" she sputtered.

But Rosie interrupted, wanting to know if he was okay

This was too much for Cat. "Rosie, who cares? What if he's seen

Jamie? Ask him about that!"

"Don't be so callous Cat, he's hurt!"

"Um, hi!" said the boy, waving his hands wildly. He winced from his injured shoulder. "I'm fine thanks, but I'll be going now." He tried to stand up, but got all twisted up and fell in the dirt, stirring up a cloud of dust. Then he became a cobra, leaning up on his front hands, carefully reaching for his jaw, and twitching when he hit a sore spot.

"Ow," he mumbled.

Rosie rushed over to him and picked up his hand, then lifted his chin up to look at his jaw. He blushed, and she blushed, turning away.

Cat was exasperated now. "Ugh, please. This is no time for grade-school crushing. Just tell us if you've seen a girl with blue hair and green eyes, super thin."

The boy was bright red now. "Other than you?"

"Yes, other than me, idiot."

Rosie frowned, clearly about to defend him (which Cat was *sure* had nothing to do with his deep blue eyes and shaggy blond hair).

But just then there was a rustling in the bushes and Cat took a step back.

"Theadore?" said an unseen voice.

Was that?

"Where are you? Who are you talking to?"

What?

The bushes parted, and a skinny pale arm reached out.

"Jamie?"

VI

Spring II

Jamie and Cat

46

Jamie

"Cat?"

Something in Jamie broke. Or went back in place, or died. Or began to live again. Cat's face crumpled, and Rosie made a sound somewhere between a squeal, a scream and a sob. Jamie noticed right away how pale Rosie looked.

Theadore wore a twisted expression of confusion and happiness. Because really, this much pure unbridled joy was contagious. Jamie stepped forward, her heart nearly beating out of her chest, her head swimming, totally overcome. But one thought shouldered every other away. A single thought.

Cat.

Her sister was *here*. She was *here*. It was like a miracle.

Almost immediately, though, self-preserving thoughts followed: Who on earth would start to look for her *here*? Unless someone had told them where to find her? Unless...Hilda! Jamie knew how easily Cat folded in the face of evil. Hilda must have persuaded her. That was the only explanation.

Still, now was not the time to conspire and doubt, now was the time to celebrate, to run to her friends. She stepped closer across the clearing towards her sister, who had silent tears running down her cheeks, hand over her mouth, face pale and pink at the same time.

Rosie dropped Theadore's hand (Wait! When had she started holding his hand?) and threw herself at Jamie, hugging her tightly.

"Never, never go away again, okay?" she said, hugging even tighter.

"I can't make promises," whispered Jamie, hugging back. Cat shied away ever so slightly.

"Cat?" said Jamie, confused. "Why are you—"

Cat turned and ran, disappearing into the leafy green.

Jamie, without thinking, dashed after her.

She could see her sister's bright pink backpack up ahead and steadily closed the gap between them, preparing to dive and tackle her. It seemed like the perfect plan, but when she leapt, Cat ducked, and Jamie did a flip in the air. Cat stopped and turned at her sister.

Jamie brushed a lock of hair out of her eyes. "Why did you come here if you're just going to run from me much less, I dunno, give me a hug?"

Cat hunched up her shoulders. "I- I just can't. I can't touch you. It's too dangerous."

"Why?"

"Because if I touch you, Hilda can find you. So please, don't come near me. Not until we're ready to fight her and Lincha okay?"

Jamie had so many questions but before she could ask even one, a terrifying shriek pierced the air. Rosie!

Jamie flew into action. Her hands glowed and she lifted up Cat in a beam of light. The two of them zoomed over the ground, covering the half mile or so they had just run in a fraction of the time.

Landing in the clearing with a thud, Cat tumbled, but Jamie landed on her bare feet without a stumble, and raced the last few feet to where Rosie lay on the ground, even paler than before, Theadore standing over her in a panic. In Rosie's outstretched palm were a pile of berries, leaking their juices like blood.

Jamie knelt down, putting her hand to Rosie's forehead. She was burning up. Suddenly Rosie's eyes snapped open, she rolled over, onto her hair, which Jamie noticed had gotten much longer, and threw up.

Gross, thought Jamie, but she held Rosie's hand. She lifted her up, and carried her back to their camp. She could feel Theadore and Cat exchange a look behind her back. But she kept walking.

* * *

Jamie dipped Rosie's head back into the creek, washing soap (that Cat had packed) out of her best friend's hair. She smiled at Rosie as she pulled her head back. Rosie smiled at her weakly. "I feel like a baby."

"Yeah, well. It's your fault for eating those berries." Jamie picked up Rosie again and carried her to the fire. It wasn't easy but was worth it because Rosie stopped shivering. Soon, she fell asleep while Jamie watched her. Cat got up and walked over to the tent, where Theadore was reading.

Jamie was staring up at the starry sky when she saw Rosie stirring in the corner of her vision.

"Jamie?" asked Rosie, sitting up a bit.

"Yeah?"

"Why do you like Tab?"

That was a stupid question. Jamie liked everything about Tab, the way her teeth were a little crooked, the way her hair always bounced even if she was standing still. She liked the way Tab talked to her, as if she were the best, most interesting person in the world. She liked her heart. She liked that Tab was smarter than her, but when they were together, they had about three brain cells combined. She even liked Tab's short temper. More than anything, she liked that Tab liked her.

"Well. I like her because I know she likes me," Jamie said.

She and Rosie were silent for a moment.

"Please stop dating her," said Rosie suddenly.

Jamie blushed, but mustered up enough courage to be mad. "It's a little late for that. Maybe if you'd have made up your mind sooner, things would have been different. Maybe next time you will."

Rosie smiled sadly. "I knew it was a long shot. But I want you to know that I love you. You're my best friend ever. And I'm sorry."

"I love you too, Rosie. You're my best friend, and I wouldn't trade you for anyone. Or anything."

"So," said Rosie, smiling mischievously, "do you forgive me?"

Jamie laughed, and they watched the stars shine.

47

Cat

I t hurt Cat to the core of her soul to hear Rosie and Jamie laughing outside, but she was good at keeping her core in check. She hugged her knees to her chest, then laid her head on top of her knees. She kicked off her boots, and noticed through her thin white socks, that practically her whole foot was charcoal black. She wanted to cry.

Seeing Jamie again hurt so much, because all she wanted was to throw her arms around her.

"Uh, you okay?"

"Gah!" Cat shrieked, jumping practically ten feet in the air. She'd completely forgotten that Theadore was in the tent with her. His voice was coming from a tiny white mouse, which freaked her out even more. "What on earth?" she whispered. Suddenly the little white mouse grew and transformed back into Theadore, and she could finally take a shallow breath.

"What—I don't..."

Theadore was red as a tomato, so she didn't finish her sentence. "No, it's fine. It's confusing. I get it. People are always confused. It's just that—well, I won't go on..." He was rambling now, but Cat found it endearing.

"No, keep talking. It's a good distraction." Cat didn't mind his embarrassment.

Given license, he basically told Cat his whole life story, which she found interesting when she listened, but that was only sporadically and when Theadore finished, she didn't realize at first and wasn't looking at him anymore but just staring out the tent flap at the shadows dancing and laughing outside.

She hugged her shoulders and continued to stare at the trees in the shadows. Theadore cleared his throat. Cat felt bad and swung around, pretending that she'd been fully listening. But the damage was done. It was written all over his face. Cat thought about saying something in her defense, but decided not to hurt him further by saying anything.

"I guess you didn't get *that* distracted anyway," he said, twisting his fingers together.

Cat sighed. "Sorry, I've just got a lot on my mind." She motioned outside but had the feeling he knew what she meant. It wasn't like she hadn't been listening at all. So she decided to ask him a couple of questions, if only to make him feel better.

"So, people hire you to spy for them?"

He nodded, obviously excited by her interest. "Yeah, I guess that's a benefit of being a freak. Actually I met Jamie on a spy job."

Now that got her attention.

"Who sent you? Why did they send you? Was it to find Jamie? Answer me, Theadore!"

He smiled a little, but Cat was dead serious.

"Theodore, answer me or I will leave you all alone to talk to yourself in this tent." He threw his hands up, in a "I surrender" position, and started explaining himself.

"It all started while I was at The Academy, and at Jamie's—well, her fake funeral. And then a couple weeks later, one of the girls who spoke asked me to follow Headmistress, and I did, and she led me to this prison place. I went back, asked the girl what to do, and she told me to see if Jamie was there, and she was. So I stayed with her for a couple of weeks until she escaped by jumping through a window—"

"WHAT?"

"Emergency measures. Anyway, I lost her because she, well, jumped out the window, and then I ran around the forest for two days and set up camp here. Which is where she found me—actually where she stabbed me in the shoulder with a stick."

Cat smiled a little, because that sounded like something Jamie would do.

"And now it's now."

Cat shuddered slightly—that was the phrase Hilda had used. "I'm just wondering," she said. "Who sent you after Hilda?"

Theadore bit his lip. "She told me never to tell you..."

"Oh, wait, I know who it is."

Theadore burst into a sweat. "Uh, no, I'm sure you don't—"

"It was Tab, wasn't it?"

Theadore went red and fumbled for words, but he couldn't keep from giving away the truth.

It turned out that Tab had sort of believed Cat's story, but in order to put her mind at rest, sent Theadore after Hilda to make sure that Cat wasn't just crazy and grieving.

And now, Cat thought, she'd find out that she wasn't crazy.

That is if they could ever find their way back.

48

Jamie

It didn't surprise Jamie that Cat had lost the taker in the middle of the forest.

She wasn't particularly angry. More worried for Cat's sake, and Kitty's, considering how many days they had left to live. Nonetheless Cat had lost it, and had to wake them up at two in the morning when she remembered where she'd left it and make them leave the camp right away so that they could find the darn thing.

Which is how they ended up trekking across the forest in the middle of the night. Rosie had recovered slightly, but Jamie still had to toss her over her shoulder and carry her. Whenever Rosie needed to eat or drink or go to the bathroom, she'd tap Jamie, which was getting old fast.

They sat on the nearest log and drank from Cat's full canteen. Rosie rested her head on Jamie's shoulder and they stared at the fading stars.

It would have been a perfect moment in another life. But considering their situation, it might have been as close they would get in this one.

Suddenly there was a loud howl and a thump and a loud smack all at once. Jamie hopped to her feet, grabbed Rosie and hustled after Cat. When they reached the place where the sound had come from, Cat was already there, standing shakily over someone's crumpled form. Theadore's eyes were wide with fear, and Cat's were wide with anger. Not good anger either. Ax murderer anger.

The crumpled figure sat up, and Cat punched him again, hitting the eye that wasn't bright red. He (now clearly a he) fell over again.

"Cat, what are you..." Jamie trailed off when she saw who it was. Despite his crumpled form and closed eyes, it was clearly Lincha. It was amazing that he was still in the forest. What had it been? Four days? And he could fly, teleport and mind read. That was slightly depressing. Jamie lunged toward her sister. "Cat, don't!" she shrieked, grabbing Cat's arm and holding her back.

When she realized what she'd just done, she dropped Cat's arm like it was flaming hot torch. But the damage was done. Her coal black arm was pale once again, and her face was full panic.

"What? *Whyyy?*" wailed Cat.

Jamie couldn't believe what she'd just done. But Cat's look of total despair was *not* helping.

"Oh my God!" Cat said. "Why did you stop me from hurting him! Why did you touch me? You wasted our one chance to survive on *him*? You put everything on the line for this evil, horrible mess of a father?"

Lincha was passed out on the ground. Theadore and Rosie were in shock. Jamie had no words.

"Jamie!"

It was like talking to a tree.

"Jamie!" This time Cat didn't sound angry. Just scared.

* * *

It was unclear exactly how Jamie, Cat, Rosie, Theadore, and Tab ended up back in the prison. All Jamie knew was that one moment, Cat was yelling at her, and the next, Headmistress Hilda had appeared out of nowhere, holding Tab by her shoulder. Then she created a little bubble and forced them in. They tried to punch and yell and fight their way out, but it was useless. Finally they'd given up, slumping down on the bubble floor.

Now they were all pretending to sleep. Not that any of them could (except for Theadore, who by some freak of nature was able to). Sometime in the dark of early early morning, Jamie began shivering. Tab scooted over, snuggling up close to share some of her body heat. "I'm still mad at you for bringing me into this," she whispered. Jamie's insides turned to jello. Her head felt light. She never thought in a million years she'd hear Tab's voice again.

"I'm so mad at myself for bringing you into this."

"You should be."

"I'm a terrible girlfriend."

"Look, it happened. What else is there to say? I was trying to contact Theadore, and Hilda caught me. You know what a terrible liar I am. I told her about my suspicions about Theadore. It wasn't great. She yelled. She was about to hit me—"

"Oh my god."

"When she got some kind of message. So she teleported us over to the forest. And, you know the rest, I guess."

Jamie started crying. Tab began crying too.

"I never thought that dating you would get this complicated. At least not this fast."

"Tab—" before Jamie could finish, Tab shifted the last few inches toward her, and kissed her.

A few things went through Jamie's head:

1: *My breath must smell awful, I haven't used a real toothbrush in a month and a half.*

2: *Why would she want to kiss me right now in this prison?*

Tab's lips were a little chapped, but not for lack of trying. It was pretty obvious that she'd worn at least ten layers of Chapstick. They were soft, and her skin was a little warm against Jamie's cheek. Her breath smelled like bubblegum and strawberries.

As awful as it was to be in this hideous Hilda-made cell, at that moment it felt like the most wonderful place in the world.

49

Cat

Cat was sure she was the only one who saw Jamie and Tab kiss.

She was thankful for that, because Rosie might have had a mental breakdown, and Theadore—well, he'd probably be really confused, and depending on the kind of boy he was, even disgusted. But she thought it was really cute, and if she hadn't been so mad, she'd have been happy.

She had kissed one boy in her old village, during a long hot day, where they had nothing to do except reenact the theater's recent production of Romeo and Juliet, and where Cat, ever the daredevil, was chosen to be Juliet alongside the town dreamboat, Jeremiah Drulop, who all the girls claimed had eyes like magic (Cat had seen magical eyes, and his were not that).

They all danced around in rags and screamed their lines in fancy renaissance language that made them laugh.

Jeremiah, it turned out, was a total wimp. He didn't have the guts to kiss Cat in front of all his friends for fear of becoming a laughingstock. So when she skipped across the square and kissed him right on the lips, he nearly fell into the fountain, and *that* made him a laughingstock.

Ever since, she'd always thought of kisses as sort of meaningless things anyone could give to anyone. Watching that ridiculous game of spin the bottle had just solidified her suspicions about kisses. But watching Jamie and Tab, kisses seemed like the most important thing in the world.

Jamie knew who she was. She knew who she liked and why. She knew what she wanted. Her place in the world was solid. She and Tab were together in every sense of the word. She was brave. More brave than Cat was for kissing Jeremiah in front of her village because she knew how people might react to her feelings and she still acted on them. Cat had been a hero for being brave enough to kiss a boy. But what if she had kissed a girl? Would everyone have celebrated? Or would she have been shunned and teased? And would her fear of those things happening make her meek? Would she have done it anyway?

She wasn't at all sure she would have.

Even though the kiss was about three seconds long at most, and possibly the first kiss they'd ever had, Cat felt like she was watching two people who'd be in love their whole lives. It made her feel a lot of things. Happy, excited, mad, sad, disgusted.

Because even though Cat had sworn up and down that she would never let her old-fashioned ideas about love get in the way of her love for her more modern sisters, she couldn't help it. Back in her time, Jamie and Tab might have ended up in jail (of course here they were, weren't they?), but growing up in that time, she knew she was a little backward. Witness her feelings about Charlotte, who'd had a daughter without a husband. Cat loved both of them to pieces, sometimes with a ferocity that made her feel that she was drowning. But her body still rejected hugging her older sister because of how sinful the reality of Kitty's existence would have been in her time.

Complicating it all right now was her righteous anger. Jamie had ruined their chances of surviving, and for what? To protect Lincha, their father? Someone who'd locked her up and conspired with the evil genius behind the downfall of every single witch and had been trying to kill them for months? It felt unfair that Jamie still got a moment of happiness while having just sealed their doom.

If Cat had found it difficult to fall asleep before, she certainly wasn't getting anywhere now. The more she watched her sister and Tab whisper and giggle and just look at each other the harder it was.

Then all of a sudden, something caught her eye. The harder she looked, the more she saw the glint. She got up and poked Jamie's shoulder.

Startled, Jamie sprung up, grabbing her arm. It hadn't exactly been a love tap.

"What? What is it? Is it because you saw us—"

Cat held up a hand. "We. Can. Discuss. That. Later."

Jamie's expression was part relief, part disbelief.

Whatever. Cat wasn't being nice anymore, they had a job to do, and this was getting in the way. "Jamie, look up there. Do you see it?"

Jamie squinted at the ceiling. The others were quietly stirring. Tab had woken up and was leaning over Jamie's shoulder.

Jamie's eyes widened. She whispered, "That's it."

"What? What is it?" asked Theadore, staring at the roof.

"It's our way out," replied Jamie and Cat at the same time.

50

Jamie

Last time in, Jamie had checked every nook and cranny of the jail cell for a way out. Looking up, there was simply an unforgiving black ceiling. But right when she looked up at where the sky would be, Jamie saw the glimmer of glass. It was undoubtedly a window. So her first instinct was to fly up there. But when she did, she hit some kind of invisible wall and boomeranged back to the floor. Cat smirked, a kind of *ha, serves you right* smile. In any other circumstance, Jamie would have punched her, but given the current circumstances, she probably did deserve it.

"Come on people, we have to get up there!" said Rosie. Tab nodded. Theadore scuffed his foot on the floor.

"Ooh!" shrieked Rosie. She placed her hands on the wall and some fire appeared. After about three minutes of them watching her, the wall started trembling. Then one of the bricks fell out of the wall and

Rosie reached out and grabbed it as a handhold. "Not what I was going for, but okay." She did the same thing again, but this time, she put her hand higher. She started to create a ladder. Everyone was getting excited. The energy was electric in the tiny cell. They had found a way out.

* * *

Jamie had gotten very good at sitting still and waiting for nothing over the past few months. But having to watch and wait, not having a role to play, herself, kind of sucked. The most annoying thing in the world was sometimes just being in a moment where you felt completely useless. Theadore in a similar role was slumped against the wall next to her, playing with a hangnail.

"Can you not maybe? That's one of my pet peeves."

"Yeah, I'm not the one who got us kidnapped."

"Hey, it's your fault Tab got in this whole mess."

Now the only sound was Rosie's fire hands and her sneakers scraping brick. As well as her nervous mumbling as she sat on the ledge that she had reached.

"You really like her huh?"

Jamie blushed.

"Um..."

"I'm really sorry I brought her into this. But please don't hate me." He was picking at his nail so much it was bleeding.

"I forgive you," said Jamie. "But could you please stop? It's making me crazy."

Theadore laughed in her ear.

"Am I being replaced right now?" asked Tab, as she walked over to them and slid down the wall. Jamie broke away from Theadore, turning to Tab.

"Like you could ever be replaced."

"So how's the escape going—besides slow?"

"Okay. Cat's getting a little tired and I'm taking a break from being a human landing pad."She grabbed Jamie's hand.

"Hmm," Jamie mused, resting her head on Tab's shoulder.

"You two are kind of barf wholesome," said Theadore.

"We'll take that as a compliment, thank you very much," replied Tab. She kissed Jamie's cheek and then stuck her tongue out at Theadore.

"Tab!" said Cat. Her face was bright red. "Come back over here. I need to make sure Rosie doesn't die." Jamie lifted her head off of Tab's shoulder, squeezed her hand and got up.

Jamie desperately wanted to talk to Cat. They had a lot of catching up to do, a lot that needed to be said, like *I miss you. What's been going on back at The Academy? How are Anna and June, the Violets, and everyone? I missed you so much it hurts. I want to yell at you. I want to punch you. I want to climb into your arms and sob until I pass out. I wish you would talk to me. I wish this could all be over.*

Theadore was biting his fingers again as he watched Rosie trembling on the ledge. Jamie was worried about her friend. The berries had taken a toll on her. She looked tired. If she fell off, Jamie was prepared to catch her like a prince in a fairytale.

"Hey, is she like, single, or?" said Theadore, quietly and quickly like the words were mice themselves.

"Who? Cat?" asked Jamie, scrunching up her nose. That would be disgusting.

"No…" he said, blushing. "*Rosie.*"

Jamie laughed. Actually laughed out loud, because that was stupid, Rosie and a mouse. As a couple. Then she realized that Cat was looking at her with a raised eyebrow. "Something you want to share?"

"Um, no, it's fine. Sorry for being loud."

Theadore was twenty-five shades of red.

Jamie was sure there was a joke to make, but she didn't want to embarrass Theadore much more than she apparently had.

Everyone turned away from them except Cat, whose gaze lingered on Jamie for a second more.

Theadore's face went back to off-white, and they sat in silence.

As the sun set, moonlight flooded the small cell, letting them know that they were running out of time.

51

Cat

Rosie had fallen asleep on the ledge. Tab was curled up, head resting on Jamie's shoulder. Theadore was slumped against the wall, head against her other shoulder. Rosie had managed to get about halfway up the wall, and pieces of broken bricks were sprinkled on the floor below. The whole cell smelled like burnt plaster and nervous sweat.

Cat couldn't fall asleep. She wanted to, but she also wanted to be awake forever. She didn't want dreams. She didn't want to leave solid ground for longer than she had to. So she stood still, just feeling her feet on the concrete. But after a while, her legs started to hurt, so she sat down and stared at her sleeping sister.

Jamie looked horrible. Cat hated to be mean, but her sister looked like a pale sickly fence post.

She was wearing what Cat assumed were Theadore's black jeans and

Theadore's t-shirt. Underneath that, Jamie was the size of a toothpick, and while she'd been a thin girl before, she had lost at least fifteen pounds since New York.

Her pageboy haircut had grown out a lot. Jamie had taken Cat's brush, and wrestled with her suddenly long locks at the creek for an hour the day before. Rosie lent her a scrunchy, and her hair was pulled back into a smooth ponytail. Her green eyes were practically bulging from their sockets, and the bags under them could carry groceries. Cat realized, while studying Jamie, that they now had the same length hair. Besides Jamie's lighter streaks, they looked exactly the same.

Cat, of course, was dressed for a party, in a black dress with a white collar (which Rosie teased made her look like Wednesday Addams, whoever that was) and purple striped stockings. Charlotte's old combat boots and Jamie's army hat completed the outfit. Despite being in such a tough situation, Cat was ready to walk the runway.

She felt herself dozing off though she didn't want to. She wanted something to rouse her, like a bright light or a loud noise. But the cell was quiet except for breathing, and dark except for the moonlight.

"Hello Cathrine," hissed a voice. Cat swiveled around, and found herself face to face with Hilda.

Yup, Cat thought, *that'll do it.*

* * *

Cat scrambled to find her pink backpack. In it was a small plastic bag, and inside that was a knife. And while Cat had never as much as stomped on a bug before she hit Lincha, she was pretty sure it wouldn't be too hard to kill this woman. Because, even though the thought scared her, she wanted Hilda to die. She really *really* wanted her to.

Hilda chuckled. "You don't have the guts, Cat. Don't pretend." She laughed again. "Oh, you kids. I hope you know you'll die in here. I'm truly sorry about Tab, Rosie and Theadore. Of course, it's your fault they'll die, but who cares about them? I'll play it off, hold funerals, add new school rules. The only one people will care about is you. You know why? Because two twins both going missing in the span of three months is suspicious."

"What's your point?" asked Cat, not putting down the knife.

"I'm giving you one last chance to leave. To take the right side. You have so much power, so much potential. You don't need your friends or her," Hilda said, pointing at Cat's friends, all of them sleeping on the ground nearby. *Her* of course meaning Jamie.

Cat could feel her heart pounding. She wondered if Hilda could hear it. "You're wrong, Hilda. I do need Jamie. More than air, more than water, more than anything including life itself. When she's not with me, I feel like I'm dead anyway. She was the piece of my life I didn't know I was missing, and when that piece is gone, it feels like I'm completely broken. And my friends. Rosie made me feel like I was part of a modern society I didn't understand. Tab's always been incredibly friendly to me, even when I was dubious about her and Jamie. Theadore cares about my sister and watched over her when I wasn't there. So you're wrong. You're wrong about it all."

She heard shifting, which probably meant her friends were waking up. But so what? She wanted to scream it from the rooftops, she needed other people. She didn't want to be alone with Hilda and Lincha in a dark desolate dungeon. She didn't want to be alone again.

"We *will* win, Hilda. Because good always wins against evil. Always. And they are not dying on my watch. So why don't you just give up? We will fight until our lungs give out. And I hope you know that—" Cat stopped speaking. Someone's hand had taken hers. It was Jamie—because of course it was.

Jamie, who forgave her after she almost got them killed. Jamie, who might have broken her heart but whom she would forever care about.

215

"Leave us alone," said Jamie. Hilda's face was smiling if a little unnerved. She regained her composure, and said: "All right then, die, that's fine with me." She raised her wand and pointed it directly at Jamie. "Too bad your story had to end this way."

Before she could shoot out her beam of deadly light, Cat lunged and stabbed her straight in the heart. Hilda's eyes rolled back. She looked utterly shocked. "Y-you..." she stuttered. "You..."

"You didn't think I had the guts?"

And just like that Hilda fell back and fizzled away like the wick of a candle that's burned up all its wax.

Hilda was dead and Cat had killed her. It had taken all her strength and resolve and left her so dizzy and weak-kneed she started crumpling to the floor. Jamie tried to catch her, but she was so weak herself that she fell down with her.

"Jamie—" said Cat, sobbing into Theadore's t-shirt.

"I know. It's okay, Cat. It's okay."

"I'm sorry," said Cat.

"I know."

The sisters hugged each other as tightly as they could, afraid to touch no more.

52

Jamie

Hilda's corpse was beginning to smell. It was like a combination of dead turtle and vulture vomit mixed with rancid month's old goat milk. They'd pushed her dead body off into a corner, but that didn't do anything to help the smell. Jamie thought they might all actually die of asphyxiation. It didn't help at all that Rosie was losing her reserve. She seemed moments away from falling off the wall, and her fire was barely a flicker now.

She'd managed to get about seven-eighths of the way up the wall, a pile of brick flakes on the floor below her. Meanwhile, Tab, who was very athletic, was trying to help, Rosie wasn't being very receptive. She was stubborn and had a lot of pride. So the two of them spent a while in a small power struggle as they both attempted to prove how they didn't need the other's help.

Theadore was also climbing, but he had settled in Tab's sweatshirt pocket, and was probably asleep too. So there was nothing for Jamie to do but sit there trying not to pass out from the smell while waiting for something to happen. Fortunately, she'd become pretty good at it. She spent about twenty minutes picking at a thread on Theadore's jeans, and she would have done it for a good thirty more if there hadn't been a sudden shriek from the top of the wall. Jamie's eyes snapped straight up. She noticed two things. First, that Rosie was practically at the top, if she were a foot taller, she could probably have touched the window. Second, Tab was holding onto a brick gap. Dangling, was a better word for it.

"Hel-hel-help," Tab stammered.

Rosie looked down at her falling friend helplessly. Jamie had seen articles about how parents had instincts and got incredible strength when their kids were in danger. Jamie didn't have any kids, of course, but something similar happened when she saw Tab hanging there about a hundred and fifty feet off the ground. A primal reaction sent her catapulting up into the sky. But in that moment she had forgotten the demon magic barrier, and it didn't care about primitive instincts. It sent her back to the ground with an inglorious thud. Fortunately, by the time she sat up and shook the cobwebs out of her head, Tab had been saved.

"Jamie, you don't need to help. It's okay," said Rosie, turning back to the wall. Fire lit, the last rung of their ladder to freedom was underway.

Jamie felt weirdly hurt. She did need to help. She hated sitting around doing nothing. She was Tab's knight in shining armor. She was supposed to have saved her. Especially because she was the one who'd gotten her into this mess.

But it didn't matter now. Because over her head, Tab was breaking open the window. They were going to be free. For the first time in months, Jamie would be free. For real.

Holy sh-

* * *

Getting four girls and a mouse up a ladder made of holes in a crumbling brick wall was harder than you might think. Rosie had already climbed out onto the roof, but Tab came down to guide Cat and Jamie up the wall. Jamie had so much adrenaline she was a whole fifteen gap-rungs above Cat and Tab.

Theadore sat poised on her shoulder like he was commanding an army, and to an extent, he was.

A laugh bubbled up in Jamie's throat. This was ridiculous. This was way too easy. They couldn't just be free. That wasn't how this worked. Although, maybe she shouldn't share this opinion with Rosie, since Jamie was sure she'd say, "Oh, it was too *easy*, huh? Who had to explode seven thousand bricks with her hands?" And she would be right.

Jamie reached the top. Cat and Tab were gaining on her, and her heart pounded away in her chest. Her fingers brushed the top of the cell. The window was spikey with broken glass, and the wooden frame was old and rotten from years left alone.

"Ready?" asked Tab, who was standing under her. She took her hand. Jamie looked at Cat.

"Go ahead," whispered Cat. Jamie gave Tab's hand a squeeze before letting go and climbing through the broken frame.

Epilogue: Full Circle

Cat climbed out the window and stood, staring at the darkening horizon. Tonight there would be no stars.

Theadore turned back into a mouse (after having stretched his legs as a human) and climbed onto Jamie's shoulder.

Rosie stood between the Novice twins and grabbed both their hands. Tab took Jamie's other hand.

"Is it summer?" Jamie asked, smelling the air, "it smells like summer."

Yes. It's summer, thought Cat, wondering if their mind-connect still worked.

Good. Jamie grinned at her.

The small mouse scratched his nose, the girl called Cat slipped away on the breeze, and the five friends breathed in the warm summer air. Because their story had just begun.

Acknowledgments

Look at you! You made it to the end of the book! Congrats.

And look at me! I finished a novel. Honestly, I have so many people to thank, and I'm going to start with my family, who inspired me so much. My mom for always having the best compliments and the best advice. And my dad for getting so committed to my novel that he basically did everything, from formatting the pages to discussing cover sizing with our (ABSOLUTELY AMAZING) cover artist. And my grandma, for having a million crazy tales to tell me, and my grandpa for his witty storytelling. For the Mailer family, a group of artists who inspire me, and the O'Neill family, for the Thanksgivings and adorable dogs.

And my friends! Annika, for inspiring the character of Anna, and also drawing and designing the cover! (I love it so much I can't even tell you.) The friends I have who didn't make it into the book, Sabrina, for laughing at my stupid jokes. Ayala, for being my confidant. Zina, for being kooky enough to balance out the terror that is middle school. Parker, for being the sweetest crazy person I've ever met. Shelby, for always making me laugh. Ellery, for being endlessly cheerful and happy for me. And of course Sarah and Mattie, my honorary sisters and partners in crime.

An extra credit to my dad for proofreading the whole thing.

And to you. For reading, enjoying, and making this worth it.

About the Author

Eden Alson was born in New York City on a beautiful cold March day in 2006. She is in the 8th Grade at 75 Morton Middle School. The Novice Twins is her first novel.